Also by Fon James

Back and Forth

A Mother, Her Son, and THE Father,
a short story appearing in *The Triumph of My Soul,*
an inspirational anthology

Forward March

A Novel

FON JAMES

Tucker House Publishing

The scriptural verses cited in this book were taken from Biblegateway.com

First Printing August 2009

ISBN-13: 978-0-9799571-2-3
ISBN-10: 0-9799571-2-3

Library of Congress Control Number: 2009931297

ATTENTION CORPORATIONS, UNIVERSITIES/COLLEGES AND PROFESSIONAL ORGANIZATIONS: Quantity discounts are available on bulk purchases of this book for educational, gift purposes, or as premiums for increasing magazine subscriptions or renewals. This is also available to various Book Clubs. Contact the Publisher for more information.

Tucker House Publishing
1795 N. Fry Road, Suite #223
Katy, TX 77449
www.tuckerhousepublishing.com
sales@tuckerhousepublishing.com

Interior and Cover designed by The Writer's Assistant www.thewritersassistant.com

Author Dedications

This book is dedicated to my beautiful daughter, Emersyn.
Mommy loves you always.

✧   ✧   ✧

I also want to dedicate this book to the
memory of my grandfather.
Rest in peace always Pa Pa.

Acknowledgments

The following words are dedicated to those who helped me on this writing journey. To my Lord and Savior Jesus Christ. Thank you Jesus for allowing me to do your work through the power of my pen. You gave me *Forward March* at the end of *Back and Forth*. I didn't know exactly what you had in store, but you sure did. I thank you for using me to let everyone know that no matter what our past, we must remember Philippians 3:13 "forgetting those things which are behind and reaching forward to those things which are ahead."

To my handsome husband, Donte. Sweetie, I appreciate your unconditional love and unconditional support. You gave me the time I needed to pen this second novel and you believed I could do it. Thank you for just being who you are to me…my everything.

To my daughter Emersyn. Mommy loves you so much. Mommy's reading fans wondered what took so long to pen this sequel and I have you to show for it. What an exceptional reason for them to wait. You are my joy and Mommy is very blessed to have you in my life.

I want to thank my parents Frank Strong and Faye McCall for their continued support. Mom, you knew having a baby would only delay my goal, not deny it. I appreciate you believing in me to get this second novel done. Dad, I know you are glad it's done so that people can stop asking you when the sequel is coming! LOL. My brother Brent, thanks for supporting me always, and for your continuing efforts of promoting my first book.

A BIG THANKS to all of my family… too numerous to name.

There are some people you connect with instantly and my writing partner and author friend, Keshia Dawn is one of those people. Thank you Keshia for pushing me to finish it. You read it as I wrote it and I appreciate your feedback, your brainstorming, the laughs, and just your pure heart of support. The writing divas are on our way!

To my editor, Shon Bacon for working your magic and making my words exactly WRITE.

To my cover and interior designer, Jessica Tilles of The Writer's Assistant. You did your thing for real Jessica. I absolutely love this cover!

Shouts out to all of my writing friends in The Writers Hut. We have to keep it coming yall.

To all my friends and social network friends on Facebook, MySpace, LinkedIN, and Twitter…keep following me and I will keep giving it to you like only I can.

To all the bookclubs who supported my first novel, thank you all so much. There were so many of you that supported me as a first time author and I am so honored that you choose my book.

I want to send a special shout out to the young ladies of the Bay Area Houston Alumnae Chapter GEMS. These young ladies are so special to me. They gave me a beautiful journal where I captured many of the notes for Forward March. Thanks ladies for helping me continue my writing journey.

Thank you to The Fort Bend Church family, especially the S.I.S. bookclub and all those who supported me and kept asking me about this book. It's here yall!

Thanks to my sorority sisters of Delta Sigma Theta Sorority, Inc., who continue to support everything I do. OO-OOP!

And finally thank you to every reader who pre-ordered this book and supported me on my first book. I love you all!

Forward March

Prologue

Journal Entry #1:

I wish he would stop trying to contact me. I am finally out of Jackson, and I still can't seem to get away from my crazy past. But now that I am living in San Francisco, my life is going to be different. I have put the past behind me. Okay, Journal, I'm lying. I have buried the past due to fear of facing it. But I am determined to put it behind me.

When I left Jackson, I was scared. Gavin and I were no longer going to be a couple. He and my best friend Chrissy were new parents to their baby girl Grace Christian and my family was on the mend from a long kept secret. I mean, I got over the fact that he slept with her and the fact that they had a baby, AND the fact that I am that child's god mother (what was I really thinking by accepting that responsibility). And then on top of all that, my folks. What can I say...it's not that I didn't get over the fact that my real mother is my aunt Jackie or that my real father is her long ago boyfriend Darnell, it's just that I grew up in a lie. Even though I pray to God everyday to help me through it, I still hold on to the fact that I am not who they said I was. My parents are Jackie Walker and Darnell Smith, not Leah and Tommie Walker. My name is still Faith Walker though. Guess since Aunt Jackie or should I say "Mom's" last name is Walker, it's okay. But I am really Faith Smith. Wow, that doesn't even sound right...Faith Smith. I can't even write it without turning up my mouth and nose.

Anyway, I haven't been home since moving out here to San Francisco to work for Elite Advertising. I know my family understands why, but I know they miss me as much as I miss them. Truth be told, I miss Gavin and Chrissy, too. Yeah, they messed up, but outside of my folks, they were two of the most important people in my life. They send me pictures of baby Grace all the time via email. I pretend like I am so busy with work and don't respond. I at least hit the button that I received it, so they know I'm getting the message. I know that's wrong, but it's weird how it all worked out with Gavin and Chrissy. I do know, however, God will continue to help see me through.

One of the pictures they sent when I first got here was the picture of all of us we took on the day I left. The entire crew was there: Me, Gavin, Chrissy, Grace and our friends Remi and Giselle. At least Remi and Giselle are doing well. I hear they're married now and living in Houston. I know I should keep in touch with them more, too, but I just try to live my life here in California, with as few reminders of my last days in Jackson, MS as possible. California is my future and I am determined to move forward.

Faith's phone buzzed. She ended her journaling session and clicked the button. She had a new email. It was him…again.

Chapter 1

"**M**s. Walker, you've done it! You scored the multimillion dollar account to do the advertising campaign for celebrity Christian artist and model Shay Praise and Pure Beauty Bars," Josie Bartrand said, shrieking. "You've only been here for a little over a year and you have managed to win one of the most sought out new accounts in the advertising industry."

"Well, Josie, it's all in a day's work. I knew I was cut out for this stuff," Faith said, blushing, "but I couldn't have done it without the entire team though. I may have come up with the ad concepts, but I definitely didn't do the art work. Malik did his thing, too, isn't that right, Malik?" she asked as if he walked by on cue past the glass doors of her 30th floor office.

Since moving from Mississippi to San Francisco, Faith had made her mark in the advertising world. Many of the employees at Elite had heard about her achievements, but she didn't want to rest on her previous accomplishments; she knew in order to move up in the ad world, she had to hit them with something big and this *big* deal was just that.

"If it ain't the big-timer who got us the big deal," Malik schmoozed. "I am just happy to be a part of *your* team, Faith. I mean, I am just elated that we work together." He laughed.

Faith and Malik had been cool since she landed in San Francisco. He had been the one to pick her up from the airport and take her around town to show her all the hot spots. As one of only a few African-Americans in the company, Elite made sure they sent someone they thought Faith could relate to. She was glad they had. There was nothing more irritating than being new and trying to get to know someone who wasn't cool or acting stuffy. Being from Mississippi, the hospitality state, Faith knew when she saw Malik, everything would be a-ok.

"Whatever, Malik! You know we couldn't have landed this deal without your magic graphic fingers. We did this together… along with the rest of the team," she said while clearing her throat and correcting her statement before someone took offense. She and Malik knew exactly who won the account with the African-American celebrity. It was them. The other people were simply on the project team.

As more people stopped by to congratulate Faith on a job well done, she realized that this career had been a great choice. While at Jackson State, she had often dreamed of landing a big time deal that would take her over the top, but she always knew she had to remain grounded, so after everyone left her office, she talked to the real man who had made this deal possible.

"Lord, it's me. I just want to thank you for this deal. I know that I couldn't have done anything without you. I thank you for putting me with the right people like Malik and for making us successful. Lord, I thank… "

Before she could finish her statement, Anastasia burst into her office.

"Faith, girl, you did your thang, huh. All that overtime with Malik really paid off. I thought you guys were just up here messing around during those late night hours."

Controlling the pupils of her eyes that she absolutely wanted to roll, Faith swiveled her chair to meet Anastasia face to face.

"Hi Anastasia," she acknowledged her presence with a dry tone. "Do you ever knock before just barging into people's offices? I could have been on the phone or something."

"You didn't look like you were doing anything to me. You looked like you were sleeping. So you're lucky I came in here before one of the managers stopped by and saw you slacking off already. Don't think because you got that new deal they're still not watching *us*."

Other than Faith and Malik, Anastasia was the other African-American at the company. She was an administrative assistant and always seemed to speak negative every chance she could get. Faith wasn't trying to hear anything negative today though. Not after landing one of the biggest deals to ever hit Elite.

"What's up, Ana? What is it that you want?"

Anastasia moved around to Faith's side of the big contemporary espresso-colored desk and sat on the edge and crossed her legs. "Look, don't be acting all brand new because you did something big. You are still black and *they* are still only going to let you go so far. You hear me, Faith. Them people will only let you go so far before they cap your butt! Look at me. Shoot, I started as a temp and I haven't gotten anything from them other than a permanent assistant job. Don't you know I gots one of them fancy degrees, too?"

Faith noticed her chest heave up and down as she breathed out a sigh. She wasn't in the mood today to hear Anastasia's, *poor-black-woman-who-can't-move-up-in-the-corporate-world* story. It was beginning to get old. Plus adding an 's' to the word "got" made her sound like she didn't have a degree.

"Ana, I appreciate you coming in to let me know that I still haven't arrived yet. I will make sure I kick my A game up and be ready for whatever the corporate big wigs try to throw my way. Thank you, girl. You really do know how to keep a girl on her toes."

"Oh, you welcome, Faith. You know I got your back. We's got to stick together, you know. That's how they do. They stick together and get each other jobs and everything. By the way, I heard that Cynthia is considering hiring a junior account executive to assist you with the new account. Think you can put in a good word for ya girl?" Anastasia popped her gum and switched it from the left to the right while waiting on an answer. Faith didn't know what to say. There was no way she was going to recommend her. What would that do to her reputation?

Everybody knew Anastasia was looking for a hand-out anytime a job came open, whether she was qualified for the job or not. She just wanted a hook-up.

Quick, Faith, think of something to get out of this, she thought while frantically wracking her brain. Just as she was about to try to think of something, Cynthia walked in. *Thank you, God, because I know you didn't want me to lie to that girl.*

"Hi, Faith," Cynthia said with a perky voice. Then she half-heartedly spoke to Anastasia, which Ana took as her cue to dip out of Faith's office.

"Just wanted to come by and commend you again on a great job." Faith noticed Anastasia still lurking by the door, making eye and hand gestures behind Cynthia as if to say with her eyes, "Hook a sistah up." Faith diverted her attention back to Cynthia just in time to nod and smile.

"So what are your plans to celebrate? We would love to take you out for drinks if you are down?" Faith hated when her managers tried to act like they were as young as she was. Cynthia was especially the worst one. She even went as far as trying to dress young with short skirts and tight suits. Cynthia was 55 years old, but unlike most women her age, she kept herself fairly well. Her short pixie-cut red hair complemented her tanned Caucasian skin and slim build. She wore the latest in designer suits and always smelled of Chanel. Jewelry was her vice. She had to wear something that clanked and banged. You could always hear her coming. It was her signature.

"Well, I was actually thinking about having a little something at my apartment tonight. You know I'm more of a homebody. You're definitely welcome to come over."

"Faith, why don't you let Elite pick up the tab on your house *partay*. You order what you want from our preferred caterer and have them deliver it. I'll have some wine delivered from our favorite winery and it'll be a blast."

"Well, I hadn't really…"

"Faith, really! Let me do this for you. You deserve so much for all your hard work. So it's a done deal. Have Anastasia email you the catering menu since she normally handles all of the catering for our office. I'll tell her what the plans are and she'll handle everything for you."

Faith hesitantly accepted. She really didn't want to have a big shindig at her place, but since Elite was picking up the tab, she may as well make the best of it. After Cynthia left, she sent Malik an email: *Guess what? Elite is picking up the tab for my get-together at the apartment. You know it's on for real now. We gone have more than soda pop. Cynthia sending the winery over. LOL.*

Malik responded almost immediately: *Oh, that's what's up fa sho. I know I am going to get my buzz on now (kidding). Because you know your boy don't drink. But do make sure you order some good food and not any of that foo-foo mess we always have here at the office. Get some wings, meatballs, egg rolls, Rotel dip. LOL. Just playing. They probably don't even have Rotel dip on that foo-foo catering menu. Lata.*

The next new message on Faith's email was from Anastasia: *I already know you gone invite your girl. Cynthia just gave me my pecking orders. Just let me know what you want me to order, and I will make it happen "BOSS LADY" LOL. Just playin, girl. Don't forget to hook a sistah up.*

Faith laughed. She had pegged Ana perfectly when she was gesturing earlier. She sent her an email back requesting the food and confirmed her attendance for the night time affair. Just as she was about to close out of her email, a new email popped up. It was him.

⌘ ⌘ ⌘

Faith left work early and rushed home. She needed to make sure her apartment was spotless for the impromptu gathering that was to begin right after work. After stacking a few industry magazines and running the swivel dust mop across her floor, Faith looked around her apartment one last time to make sure everything was in its rightful place. Even though she was only entertaining a few friends and coworkers, she wanted to make sure everything looked up to par in her loft.

Since moving to San Francisco, she had become somewhat of a minimalist. Her simple platform bed and loft furniture she picked out from IKEA in nearby Emeryville made her feel as if her life was simple and uncluttered. Gone were the cluttered dorm day madness of college and the old school bedding at her aunt Jackie's home back in Mississippi.

Her bedroom, which could be seen from every spot in the 22nd floor loft was pure white. As a part of her moving forward in life from all the craziness and drama she left behind, she wanted a fresh start. And what better way to have a fresh start than with pure white. She reflected on the cross-stitched verse she had sitting in a frame on her nightstand. Isaiah 1:18 - "Come now, let's settle this," says the LORD. "Though your sins are like scarlet, I will make them as white as snow. Though they are red like crimson, I will make them as white as wool."

That was her new theme in life...even though she had gone back and forth and sinned while in Mississippi, her trek to California was the beginning of a purification journey. Just as she was about to straighten the moveable partition that served as a wall separator when she wanted to block off areas of her loft, the doorbell rang.

"Hey, Shawny, what's the dill, pickle?"

"You know you got it, baby girl," Shawny replied as he kissed Faith and handed her the large colored bouquet of assorted flowers he was carrying.

"Shawny, are these for me? You shouldn't have." Faith admired the beautiful bouquet.

"Well actually, I didn't." He laughed, but then quickly cut it off when Faith frowned at him. "Stop looking like that, baby girl. Don't act like I wouldn't buy you flowers because you know I would, but these ain't from me. Maybe you got some kinda secret admirer because they were just sitting at your door when I came up. Maybe there's a card or something tucked in there."

Faith smelled the flowers and looked for a card. Before she could even find the small card hidden beneath the bouquet, she surmised that it was probably from Elite. They had really been going all out on the congratulations today and flowers wouldn't be a far departure from them trying to let her know how much they appreciated her getting them the big account. She reached for the card as her cell phone rang.

"Shawny, can you open the card and see who sent these flowers? This may be somebody on the phone from my job trying to find my place."

Shawny opened the card and read the message. He rolled his eyes and looked to see if Faith was still on the phone. "This dude never stops," he silently mouthed. Just as he was about to put the card back in the little envelope, Faith reappeared.

"So who's it from? Elite?"

"Nah, baby girl, but before I give it to you, I want you to promise me that you are not going to overreact or get mad. Today is a great day and we are celebrating all that you have achieved since you've moved out here to Cali, so promise me."

"Look, Shawny, I can't promise you anything until I see the card. So hand it over."

Shawny reluctantly handed over the card and watched Faith as she opened the envelope and slid out the small card. It read: *Congratulations on your success! I always knew you would do something big in*

California. I miss you so much. Please call me or accept my emails. I love you, baby. I do still love you, Faith. Gavin.

Faith let out a long sigh. She had been doing a great job avoiding him and his messages. She thought he had caught the clue when she didn't respond to any of his *reach-out* tactics.

"See that's why I wanted you to promise me."

"Why does he keep doing this? I am done. Doesn't my lack of communication say that loud and clear?"

Faith felt herself getting flustered, and as he had done since they both moved to California, Shawny wrapped his arms around her and comforted her.

"Thank you so much for always being there for me when I need you most, Chrishawn Jackson."

The doorbell rang again and this time it was the food and wine being delivered. Faith let them set up in her kitchen and not long after the food arrived, most of her guests showed up to celebrate her latest accomplishment. While entertaining her friends and coworkers, she kept noticing the bouquet in the corner of her eye. It was so colorful against all the white, she couldn't miss it. The flowers, as beautiful as they were, was a bold and ugly reminder of her past, now sitting in a large room filled with her present.

How did he even find out about my deal? she thought. *I know they sent out a press release, but he couldn't have possibly found out unless he was stalking me or something. Maybe if I just respond to his reach-outs and let him know that I would prefer he not contact me, he will catch the hint and leave me alone.*

The party was fun and Faith felt good about celebrating her new accomplishments with her coworkers and friends. It was still pretty early after everyone left and since she was on Pacific Time, Faith decided to call her parents and share her good news. She had put it off for the day just to bask in her achievements, but now it was time to call home, both homes.

"Hey, Momma, what you are up to?"

Leah and Tommie were lying on the couch watching a movie when Faith called and immediately paused the movie when they heard her voice.

"Hey, Faith, girl it is so good to hear from you. Hold on and let me put the phone on speaker so that your daddy can hear you." See it was things like that that still made Faith feel uneasy. Tommie wasn't her daddy.

"Push past it, Faith, and let it go," she heard the voice in her head whisper.

"Can you hear us, baby?"

"Yep, I can hear y'all loud and clear. Move away from the mouthpiece some because I can hear you breathing and everything." Faith laughed.

"That's your daddy, Faith. He's all up in the phone. Move over some, Tommie, so we can both talk to the girl. You know she don't call us that much."

And there it was. Faith knew it was coming sooner or later. She knew they wanted to hear from her more often, but it was what it was.

"Well anyway, guys, I just called to tell you all my good news."

"Good news, what's good, baby girl," Tommie chimed in.

"Well Daaa," Faith paused before she completed the word Daddy. "Uh, well basically, y'all I got us a million dollar account at work."

"What you say! Hot dog, Faith! That's our girl. I knew you were over there doing your thing on the West Coast. That's why I told your daddy you don't have time to be calling us everyday. That is truly awesome, honey. So what does that mean? Are you getting a raise, a bonus, a promotion?"

"Whoa, slow down, y'all with all the questions." Faith realized that saying *y'all* helped her not refer to Tommie and Leah Walker as

Momma and Daddy. "I am definitely getting a bonus and I hope that my work will eventually land me a promotion and fa sho a raise."

"We are so proud of you right now, Faith. Have you called Jackie yet?"

"No, I haven't called her yet. I was planning on doing that after I talked to y'all first."

"Okay, well we won't hold you because I know she will want to hear this great news. Matter of fact, she will probably share her great news with you, too."

"What great news?

"We'll let her tell you," they said in unison.

"What? Can't y'all tell me?" Faith hated surprises.

After several attempts, Faith gave up and decided to call Aunt Jackie herself. She said goodbye and immediately dialed the familiar number.

Chapter 2

"I'm sorry, Mrs. Aguilar, but the test is negative," the nurse spoke with a sad tone. "But you're young, so I am sure it will happen for you soon." Her tone had turned chipper just that fast.

Giselle looked at the picture of her husband on her desk. Her face surely showed the disappointment, but luckily no one was around her cubicle to see the grim look she was now sporting. She just *knew* she was pregnant this time. "Okay, well thank you for the call, Brenda. And I appreciate your encouragement, too," she added, not wanting her nurse to think that she was ungrateful.

"Mrs. Aguilar, you and that husband of yours just keep on trying and it will happen in God's timing."

"Thanks again, Brenda."

Giselle placed the phone in the cradle and hung her head low. "Why not now, God?" She questioned God and knew she shouldn't have, but she just couldn't resist. "Lord, how long do I have to wait to become a mother?" Just as she was about to utter another question, her phone rang.

"Houston Heights Publishing, this is Giselle Aguilar speaking."

"Hey, baby, it's me. How are you doing today?"

"I was just about to call you, Remi. I just got a call from the doctor's office. It's a no-go, again."

Sucking his teeth, Remi expressed his disappointment about the news. "Awe man babe, I really thought we would hear positive results this time. Did the nurse say anything about what we can do?"

"Nope, she just said the usual. I'm young and it will happen in God's timing. Remi, to be honest, I am tired of hearing that." Giselle began to cry. "I mean, when *is* it going to be the right time? We both have good jobs. We are settled here in Houston. We have a beautiful home thanks to your dad, and our finances are solid. What else do we need? I am so sick of that nurse telling me that I am young. I know that. And I am Christian, so I know everything will happen in God's timing, I just thought this *was* His timing."

"G, babe, just calm down. It's going to be okay. I don't want you getting all upset. The nurse is right though. Everything will happen when God wants it to happen. We just gotta hold on, okay, babe?"

"I'm just tired of holding, Remi." She continued to cry. "We have been trying since our honeymoon night. I mean, we weren't as ready then as we are now, but that's even more reason why I don't understand why not now."

Giselle didn't realize how loud she had gotten while talking to Remi and one of her co-workers heard her as she was walking by.

"Remi, I just feel like my faith is waning. What did I do to not deserve to be pregnant right now?"

"Giselle, now you know you didn't do anything. You are a strong Christian woman. Don't let Satan get you down with this news. We're going to have a baby in due time. Let's not focus on the negative results, okay? When you get home, let's go out to dinner, have a little wine, and get our minds off of this stuff. There's a new restaurant in Houston that I want to try out with my favorite girl."

"Remi, I am your only girl," Giselle reminded him with a smile that seemed to have come out of nowhere. Once again her husband had lifted her spirits. She loved spending time with her beau, and trying a new eating spot would sure cheer her up. It had become her and Remi's favorite thing to do on the weekends since moving to Houston.

"And you know you are, girl. I just wanted to make you smile by saying that. I'll see you soon, okay. I gotta make a few client calls before I leave the office and my dad wants to see me before I leave, too."

"All right, tell Dad I said hi."

"Sure thing, babe. Lata."

Giselle kept staring at the picture of Remi on her desk. He was so handsome and she knew their baby would be so beautiful. Remi was half black, half Hispanic and had the most beautiful jet black curly hair. His biracial skin tone coupled with her smooth chocolate skin was baby celebrity genes in the making. She had already looked up modeling agencies in Houston because she knew their baby would be the next Nike or Gap baby. As she smiled about the possibilities, her co-worker interrupted her daydream.

"Hey, girl, is everything okay? I sort of overheard you on the phone and I just wanted to check on you and make sure that you all right. I wasn't trying to eavesdrop, but you got a little loud."

"Oh, hey Chaka. Girl yeah, I'm cool. I just got a call from the nurse and my pregnancy test results were negative again. But I'm okay. My husband has a way of calming me down, thank goodness."

"I'm sorry to hear that, Giselle. Well, you know it's going to happen, so you just gotta keep on trying. And hey, you can have fun while trying…that's the best part!" The two laughed as Chaka raised her eyebrows and did a quick shimmy to her own beat.

"Thanks, Chaka. I'm just so ready to have his baby and be a mommy. But you're exactly right. I just got to keep trying and have faith that God will deliver in His time."

"Well I am glad to see that your spirits are up. Look, did you meet the new chick in production? She's absolutely gorgeous girl, and I don't usually comment on women. But she's the new production manager and according to the rumor mill, she got her stuff together. They didn't bring her over here to meet you?"

Chaka and Giselle started at Houston Heights together. Chaka, not one to ever hold her tongue about any subject, was a Jill Scott look-a-like. She and Giselle hit it off on their first day of training.

"Nah, girl, I didn't meet her. I have been in marketing meetings most of the day, so they may have brought her over and I wasn't here."

"Well come on, let me introduce you to her. She seems to be a really nice girl. Plus, I need another reason to go over there and get another cookie. You know anytime somebody new starts we got to have food at this company."

Giselle and Chaka made their way through the maze of light khaki colored cubicles to meet Reyna Reynolds.

"Reyna, this is Giselle Aguilar, our marketing associate," Chaka introduced. "She's been in meetings all day and didn't get a chance to meet you."

Giselle smiled and extended her hand to Reyna. She noticed how beautiful Reyna was, just as Chaka had mentioned. She was more of an exotic beauty. Her hair was a silky jet black and she looked as if she worked out every day, not your normal three times a week routine. She had a small mole right above her top lip, sort of like the smooth dot on an exclamation point of beauty. *She had to be biracial or have some Indian or New Orleans French connection going on,* Giselle thought.

"Welcome to Houston Heights, Reyna. It's a pleasure to meet you," she said.

"Giselle, is it?"

"Yes, that's it." Giselle hesitantly replied, noticing the snide tone when Reyna confirmed her name.

"Oh, nice to make your acquaintance."

There it was again Giselle noticed. *Why is this girl tripping? She just met me.*

"Well, I work in marketing so I am sure we'll be seeing a lot of each other. If you need anything, please feel free to let me know. I sit right over there near the copy room," Giselle pointed.

"Oh. Okay. Thanks." Reyna didn't express a hint of excitement.

Giselle and Chaka both left Reyna's desk, but not before Chaka could grab a couple of chocolate chip cookies from the file cabinet next to Reyna's desk.

"Okay, is it just me or did she have a straight up attitude?" Giselle quizzed.

Chaka stuffed the cookie into her mouth before answering.

"Yeah, girl. Excuse my ghetto, but she was just stank! I don't know much about the chick, but I heard that she is smart as a whip and graduated from Xavier University in New Orleans. But of course that doesn't give you a pass on niceness. But the funny thing is, she didn't have that stank attitude earlier today. It was just when she met you, Giselle."

"Humph, that's weird. You *know* I don't know her. I just moved to Houston not too long ago, so I am still meeting people."

"Yeah I know. Maybe she just hating on you. She's probably used to being the most beautiful girl in the room. You, Ms. Mississippi, are giving her a run for her money."

"Girl, you are so funny, and thanks for the compliment. You're right, she's a very pretty girl, but her attitude is U-G-L-Y!" They both laughed at Giselle mocking the old high school cheer, You UGLY.

Reyna had made her way through the maze and was now standing in the copy room with her ear hard pressed on the conversation between Giselle and Chaka.

"Those heifers better watch themselves. They don't know what I'm about. And that Giselle with her *pretty* self will get hers soon enough," she silently mouthed.

⊱   ⊱   ⊱

"Hey, Dad, I just got the HUD paperwork for the River Oaks deal. I need to fax over a few things for the Haydes to sign and I think this one can be closed by the end of next week."

"That's awesome, son. It hasn't taken you anytime to get your feet wet in this real estate game. You're going to be stunting like your daddy real soon." His father laughed while making reference to one of rapper Lil Wayne's album titles.

"See there you go trying to keep up with my age group."

"Well, son, what can I say," he replied in his best Jimmie "JJ" Walker from Good Times, imitation.

Mr. Aguilar's cell phone rang.

"This is Rohan Aguilar, how can I help you?"

"Hey, Mr. Aguilar, is now a good time to talk?"

Nervously fidgeting in his seat when he recognized the female voice on the other end, he quickly replied, "Actually, I am in a meeting. Is it possible for me to call you back?"

Remi was waving his arms as if to say you can take the call, but his father waved him off.

"Sure, you know the number, Mr. Aguilar. I'll await your call back."

"Yep, sure thing. I will give you a call back today."

"I bet you will."

And with the call going dead, Rohan hung up the phone and focused his attention back to Remi.

"Dad, you could have taken that call. We can talk later."

"No, son, I will call them back. I wanted to talk to you now about this new deal we got out in the suburb of Katy. This might take my company over the top. There is some new development out there and this custom builder may want us to be the realtor of choice to sell all of his new custom homes. The houses will range in price from $500k to over $3 million."

"Whoa, now that's big bucks, Dad. So where do I fit into this?"

"Well that's what I want to talk to you about. I told the owner of Mayhorn Custom Homes that I want my son to run this project and he agreed. He's actually grooming his son to run the Katy development project as well, so both of you youngsters will need to meet real soon. I was wondering if we could all do lunch next Monday if you are free."

"Most definitely. This is great."

"I thought you'd think so. Son, you've got a good head on your shoulders, and I know you will do well on this project."

"Thanks for the vote of confidence, Dad. I got a good teacher." Remi winked.

"Yep, you do," his father replied with cockiness. "So how's my daughter-in-law? Are you keeping her happy?"

"As happy as I can. She was a little down today because we got the news that the test results were negative again. To tell you the truth, I was disappointed myself, but I had to be strong for her, you know. I know we just gotta keep trying. Hopefully there's nothing wrong with me and my shooters."

"Awe, son, I know there ain't nothing wrong with your shooters."

"How can you be so sure, Dad?" He laughed.

"You're an Aguilar. We are always cocked and fully loaded. *And* we don't miss or shoot blanks. We're fruitful men."

"You sound so sure of yourself. And what do you mean fruitful? I *am* your only child, right? Please don't be telling me I got a sister or another brother around here somewhere. What am I saying? I would be talking to your grave if that were the case because you know Mom would be in your tail." Remi snickered.

"Now, son, you know you right. Your mother is my mocha angel, and I would never do anything that is not pleasing to her. We've been married a long time and that woman still has the same sparkle she had when I met her. She's just a classy lady all around and I recognize what I got, son."

"I hear that, Dad. I have always admired you and Mom and I can only pray that me and Giselle have that kind of lasting love. She's my heart."

"You keep making her happy. Y'all kids are going to do just fine."

"Kids? Come on, Dad. We are adults trying to have a kid. You and Mom will never let me grow up will you?" He stood and adjusted his designer suit coat. Rohan looked at his son and smiled in admiration. He and Charlotta had done well with their only son.

"Yeah, whatever, lil man," he replied playfully.

"All right, Dad, I will holla at you later, old man."

"I got your old man." His father rubbed his slightly gray goatee. "You hope you look as debonair as I do at 55." Rohan ran his hair through his black curly locks. "Don't nothing get old but clothes…you hear me, boy. Nothing but clothes."

The two shared a laugh before Remi left. He was glad he had decided to move back home to Houston to work for his dad's real estate firm. It was one of the top firms in Texas, and he knew it would only be a matter of time and experience before he would be running the entire show. His dad was retiring in five years, and Remi was the heir apparent to the real estate throne.

No sooner than Remi got out of Rohan's office, he returned the phone call from earlier.

"Hey, what is that you need now?"

"Well, hello to you too, Mr. Aguilar."

"Look, I am not feeling the small talk. I've got business to take care of. What is it?"

"Okay, Okay. You don't have to rush me. I was thinking…"

Rohan took a long breath to calm his nerves. He hated when she was *thinking*.

"I've decided to put Recio in that new private school and of course the money that you give me won't cover it. Sooo, I need more."

Rohan gritted his teeth. "How much more?" he asked with stern lips.

"I think the lady told me it's going to be around $15,000 a year or something like that. Plus money for uniforms, shoes to match, etc. etc. etc."

"What's wrong with the school that Recio is in now? The boy is only three years old."

"Correction. He's almost four. And plus I want the best for my baby. Don't you want what's best for your blood?"

"Of course I do, but a three-year-old, *excuse me,* almost four-year-old going to a $15,000 a year school is absolutely absurd."

"Well, Mr. Aguilar, the way I see it, we either *do* what I want or I *say* what I want to whomever I want…if you know what I mean."

Rohan loosened the silk neck tie that had now begun to feel like a noose around his neck.

"Fine! Where do I send the damn check?" he asked.

"Oh, you can make it out to me and I will handle it."

"Now you know good and darn well I am not making it out to you. I will pay for the boy's schooling, but I am only making the check out to the school. So who do I make it out to?"

"Whatever, have it your way. Make it out to Dreshall Prep Academy."

"I will have the check sent via courier to you today. Next time you get to thinking, STOP!"

Rohan hung up the phone. He massaged his temples and took long deep breaths. This madness was the culprit to his graying goatee.

After writing the check out from his private account, Rohan called the courier service.

"Yes, I need a delivery made to 2777 Ashby Lane today. Yes, charge it to the same account as always."

After three years of secrecy, the pressure to keep up with her demands was weighing on him.

I got to figure out a way to stop this, he thought. *Especially now that Remi is back home.*

Chapter 3

Faith immediately dialed Jackie's phone number. She was so anxious to hear her news she dialed the wrong number the first time.

"Faith, is that you?" Jackie picked up the phone excitedly.

"I see you still excited to have Caller ID on all your phones," Faith teased.

"Girl, this is the best thing since they made the TV colorized. What's my girl doing in big Cali? I haven't heard from you in a long while. I was going to call you, but I said nope, when she get ready to talk, Miss Hot Pocket will call me." Jackie had been calling Faith Miss Hot Pocket most of her life. She had come to adore the nickname, but after she started gaining weight, she wanted to switch it to Lean Pocket because that's what she needed to be eating.

"Well, I just wanted to call you and tell you my good news."

"What? What is it, girl? Spill it? You know I don't like surprises," she said in a hurried tone.

Like mother like daughter, Faith thought.

"I got my company a multimillion dollar account with Christian artist Shay Praise!" Just saying it made Faith poke her chest out. It *was* a big deal and she knew it.

"What – you – say!" Jackie shouted with her southern drawl. "That's my baby. Girl, you got Shay Praise. Now you know you done hit the big league now. Have you met her yet? What's the campaign going to be? What will she be advertising? When will I see a commercial or print ad? How did you do it, baby? What was your pitch?"

"Aunt Jackie, slow your roll with all the questions. Dang, you would think you work in advertising asking me all that." Faith laughed. "I see my hanging out with you and sharing every detail about my advertising work when I was in Mississippi made you a mini-expert."

"Sure did. So when will I see something?"

"Soon enough. We are still working on everything now, but they loved all of the prototypes we developed. Oh yeah, she's going to be advertising Pure Beauty bars. We got deals with all the African American magazines, including your favorite…"

"Essence!" Jackie shrieked before Faith could finish her sentence. "Your work is going to be in Essence? Oooh Faith, I am so proud of you!"

"Thanks Aunt Jackie, but look, Momma and Daddy told me that you had some news so *you* spill the beans before my brain formulates a headache from me trying to figure out what's going on with you."

"Humph, if you would call me, sometimes you would know what's going on."

"Okay, whatever, just tell me already. Geez Louise, y'all know I hate surprises."

"Me too. Ain't that funny how we both hate…"

Faith cut her off. "Aunt Jackie!" she screamed.

"All right. Well, are you sitting down?"

"Yeah," Faith lied to keep her moving with the story.

"You know me and Darnell have been hanging out for the past year since we reconnected right before you left home."

Faith took a seat on the sofa. Her mind started moving faster than her aunt's words and she just knew she wasn't about to hear what her Speedy Gonzales brain had concocted.

"He proposed, Faith. Your father and I are getting married!"

Yep, there it was. Just as she figured from the tone in her aunt's overly excited voice.

"Faith? You still there?" Jackie couldn't hear anything on the other end of the phone.

Faith closed her eyes. Now it was sure to be official. Her real parents, Aunt Jackie and Darnell Smith were getting married. She squeezed her temples to ward off the headache that was coming. She wasn't ready to deal with this. That's why she had avoided home as much as possible. She could hear Jackie on the phone calling her name, but she had zoned out. She began imagining coming home to her parents' home, not Tommie and Leah, the two people she knew as Momma and Daddy, but Jackie and Darnell, her biological parents. The phrase going home took on a whole new meaning. What was that going to be like?

"Faith Walker, answer me before I call the police and have them come to that fancy loft of yours in San Francisco to check on you."

Faith zoned back into the conversation when she heard Jackie getting worried.

"I'm here, I'm here. Calm down."

"Girl, you scared me. What is wrong with you? Aren't you happy for me?"

"Yes, Aunt Jackie, I mean Mom. Ugh, see therein lie the problem. I am just not ready to deal with my identity crisis right now. I was simply calling to share my good news and you drop this on me."

"Faith, sweetie, I know you are still trying to come to grips with everything we revealed to you before you left home, but honey, like we all have done…it's time for you to move forward. You now know the truth and we have to all live our lives in this new truth."

"That's easy for you to say. You're not the one who was lied to for over 20 years. You're the one who did the lying. I mean, I forgive everybody because I know it was for a good cause, but don't expect me to just up and change and start calling you and Darnell Mom and Dad, and Momma and Daddy, Leah and Tommie. It's not that easy. Plus it's so freaking awkward when I talk to y'all that it stresses me out. That's why I haven't called you."

"Avoiding the issue and not dealing with it head on doesn't ever resolve anything, Faith. You already know this. Have you still been going to church with Chrishawn every Sunday? I hope so because I know you know once you give it over to God, then you are not to take it back. You do know that, right?"

"Yes, ma'am I know that. But it's just a struggle to think about it all. I don't know how to respond to it. That's why I pour myself into my work. I'd rather just not deal with it now."

"Honey, it's been a year already. Seriously, Faith, give it to God and get over it already. Your father and I are about to get married and we want you to be very much a part of our lives. Yes, it's a different situation than most people have to face, but with God anything is possible."

"Okay, well I need to get ready for tomorrow. I hate to cut the conversation short, but we've been on here a while now anyway, so I will talk to you later."

"You're doing it again, Faith. You're running away. Stop running and pray to God. Let's pray right now."

Faith began to cry as her aunt went into prayer. She knew that the time would come where she would have to deal with this part of her life. She just wanted it to be on her terms.

"Thanks, Aunt Jackie. I really needed that."

"Faith, if you want to call me Aunt Jackie for the rest of your life, that will be fine with me. I am sure Darnell won't mind if you called him Darnell. Whatever you're comfortable with is fine with us. The most important thing is that you know whose you are...and that's a child of God first and foremost."

"Thanks, Mom." Faith ended the call and went to her bedside table to grab her journal. She needed to write.

Lord, I thank you for making me into the unique being that I am. Although I wasn't quite ready to deal with this identity crisis, you've

*shown me that I never have to wonder who I am because I am yours,
no matter who my parents are. I thank you for allowing me to grow up
in a nurturing home with parents who loved me. I thank you for Aunt
Jackie who treated me like the daughter I really was to her. I thank you
that I will get a chance to get to know my real father.*

*But I need your strength to help me. I can't do anything without you.
It was you that guided me when I worked on the new deal with Shay
Praise. It was you that helped me to forgive Gavin and Chrissy. It was
you that brought a strong Christian man into my life with Chrishawn.
Thank you, Lord. Thank you for…*

Faith was interrupted by her cell phone.

"Faith, I forgot to tell you to block off October for the wedding,"
Jackie announced.

"What? That's only two months away. How are you going to plan
a wedding that fast?"

"Baby, my wedding is already planned. Every since I was teenager
I knew what kind of wedding I wanted. I have a vision board with my
dress, my colors, everything. I had to make a few modifications to
update some stuff, but otherwise, I already got the vision God gave me
and it's about to come to pass."

"Oh…okay then. When in October?" Faith quizzed. She couldn't
pull up her calendar on her blackberry since she was talking on it. She
knew that the launch festivities for Shay Praise were in August and her
work projects would be functioning on auto by September.

"It will be the third Friday in October. We're having a night time
wedding. Oh yeah, you need to try on your dress. My colors are
Tiffany blue and silver. I already have a dress picked out for you, but
since I don't know what size you are anymore because I haven't seen
nay picture of your butt since you been in Cali AND because you act
like you can't come home, you can go to Nordstrom and try it on. It's
off the rack and I already checked; they have a size 4 and size 6 at the
one near you."

"Wow, you do have this all worked out. Okay, I will go by the store tomorrow. What brand is the dress and what does it look like?"

"I'll email you everything. You're going to love the flowers we picked out. It's going to be gorgeous, Faith. Oh, I am getting giddy just thinking about it. Just check your email shortly. By the way, you know you are going to be one of my maids, right? You're not just *attending*."

Faith shut her lids for a quick second and imagined walking down the aisle at her mom and dad's wedding. She couldn't fathom it. All she could see in her dreams was her walking down the aisle in a beautiful white gown. She smiled to herself.

"Faith, girl I d'clare. You act like you can't hear me sometimes."

"I hear you. Send me the email and I will check everything out. And Aunt Jackie, I mean Mom, I really am happy for you and Darnell. Really, I am."

"Thank you, baby. I prayed God would help you accept it and I see He is still in the blessing and prayer answering business."

Just as they were about to hang up, Jackie added, "Oh yeah, Faith, I saw Chrissy at church last Sunday and she told me to tell you hi and that you need to call her. She's got some news to share with you."

"Great, more news," Faith replied dryly while rolling her eyes.

"You just call the girl and see what's going on. She wouldn't tell me and you know I want to know, too." Jackie laughed. "I did tell her about the wedding and invited her, Gavin and the baby to come. I saw that baby Sunday and my Lord she looks just like Gavin. She's the cutest thing. I hope you didn't mind me inviting them."

"Hey, it sounds like a done deal already, so even if I did mind, I can't object now."

"Good. Now if I can just get you to get in contact with Remi and Giselle, I will have my list of invites completed. I started to look them up in Houston, but this will give you an opportunity to call them. I know you haven't talked to them either."

"You're right. I haven't talked to anybody and that's pretty much how I wanted it to stay until I was ready, but after our conversation, I think I am ready to face my friends. I wonder what's going on with Chrissy."

"Why don't you hang up from me and call her and find out. Then call me back and fill me in. Oh yeah, she gave me her new number. Jot this down."

Faith took the number down. It was a New York area code. What was that about?

Chapter 4

"Hey, Ma, where are you?"

Chrissy walked into the all familiar home and noticed how clean and nice it was. Her mom had been redecorating for the last month and she really liked the new look. All of the old furniture with smoke stains had been replaced with new modern pieces. Her mother had decided that after the break up with her ex-boyfriend Darnell, she needed to start making some changes with herself. She stopped smoking and threw out anything that smelled liked smoke.

"We back here, Chrissy. I was just cleaning up Lil Ms. Gracie pooh. She just ate, with her hands of course. Chile, she had spaghetti everywhere. Then, you know what came after she ate." She laughed.

Chrissy walked back to her old room. Her mom had converted it to a baby room for Grace. It was still red and white like when Chrissy grew up there, but all the lady bug themed baby stuff had the room completely transformed. Chrissy reminisced and thought briefly how it had been this very room where she had tried to abort Grace by taking pain pills. *Thank you God that I failed.*

"Hey, Momma's punkin seed…what have you been doing today? Have you been a good girl for your G-Ma?" Chrissy smiled at her daughter, who was grinning and smiling back at her. She could tell Grace was happy to see her. She walked over and took her from her mother who had just snapped her pink pants back together from the diaper change.

"I'm sure going to miss this."

"Miss what, Chris? I know you not fretting over Grace having your room. I already told you…"

"I talked to the fashion house today, Ma, and it looks like I will be moving to New York sooner than later."

Charnese looked at her daughter in shock, and then slowly revealed a smile. She couldn't believe her daughter was going to be moving from Mississippi all the way to the big city of New York. She was happy for her achieving so much after having had Grace, but it was a bittersweet happiness she had for her only daughter.

"But I thought you said you would be working from home for at least the rest of this year."

"They want me to go ahead and come up there. It will be better for me to actually be there anyway. Some of the marketing work I have done telecommuting has been hectic to say the least because of my locale. But you know we agreed that all parties would make sure I was the best fit for the job before I made the big move.

"Plus having a child changes everything and I didn't want to be uprooting Grace before I got settled into this new company. Anyway, I'm so excited, Ma. We got a new line of young women's clothes that we are pushing into the major department stores and I've seen the pieces. They are HOT!"

"You already know you can hook your Ma up because I got to be fly."

"Ma, notice I said they are for *young women*."

"And *I* said, you already know you can hook your Ma up. I'm as young as they come, baby doll. Don't get it, twisted sister. I am young, foot loose and fancy free. Hollaaaaaaa!"

"You know you watch too much TV. Stay off of BET before you hurt yourself." Chrissy laughed.

"So have you told Gavin about the move yet?" her mother asked. Grace heard her father's name and started yelling Da Da."

"Baby, your Da Da ain't here," Charnese said. "He probably somewhere trying to call Faith with his no good a…"

"Ma, don't be cursing around Grace. I told you about that. I don't want her growing up hood like me and Chrishawn did."

"Hood? Girl, please. Y'all are doing just fine. You about to be on the East Coast working for a new and upcoming African American fashion house and your brother Shawny is on the West Coast doing his church thing. I think I did a'ight if I say so myself." She brushed her shoulders.

"Yeah, that's because we overcame all the drama. Thank God I started going to church with Faith; otherwise, who knows what I would be worshipping right about now."

"Have you told Gavin yet is the question, smarty arty?"

"Nah, I haven't. I sent him a text message once I got the news about the move. I'm waiting for him to call me back. But really, Ma, it doesn't matter what he says. I'm going to New York and Grace is going with me. They have a daycare at my job and she will be with me. Plus, we got our cousins Derek and Davina out there, and they have already said they want to be a part of our lives. So if I have to work on weekends, which I may have to do during some of the launch parties, then they are both willing to watch Grace. It's all going to work out for me and my baby."

"I know it's going to work out, baby. I just hate that you are taking my grandbaby all the way to New York."

"You just gone have to get your flights together and come visit us often, that's all."

"Yeah, you right. Both of my babies are going to be gone now. What will I do with myself? Gracie pooh has been my life since you've been trying to get your career off the ground. Now I will have to figure out what I will do with my time."

"I'm sure you'll figure out something, Ma. You've never been one to be a homebody. Maybe you can start your daycare business like you talked about doing when you first started keeping Grace. Lord knows we could use some quality daycare in the neighborhood."

"That's a great idea, baby. I'm going to look into that. By the way, did you hear the latest news?"

"No, what happened?" Chrissy replied, overly anxious to hear her mother's gossip.

"Chile, I heard that my ex boyfriend, you know, your friend Faith's *real* father, is getting married."

"Oh, I already knew that, Ma. I thought you were about to tell me something good and juicy."

"Wait a minute, your behind knew and didn't tell me? What kind of shitzu is that?"

"Ma, saying shitzu is just like cursing, so please stop that. But yeah, I saw Ms. Walker at church the other Sunday and she told me the good news. I didn't think you cared since you and Darnell haven't spoken to each other since he found out about Faith being his daughter."

"I don't care. I just thought you would have told me or asked if I knew. Humph, he gone marry old Jackie, huh. Well good for them. Now they can be one big happy family when Faith comes home. Has that child come home yet since she been in Cali? Shawny be acting funny when I ask about her. Like he don't want to tell me nothing."

"Probably because he doesn't, Ma. You know he and Faith are very close and you got a big mouth. And no she hasn't come home since she left. But I know she got to be coming to the wedding. I told Jackie to tell her to call me. I wanted to tell her about my working for All Black Designs. I am hoping she and I can work together in the future with her doing advertising work in the multicultural markets."

"So she hasn't called you yet?"

"Nope, but I am hopeful she will. I am hoping that now that we are all moving on with our lives, she and I can try to at least have a semi-decent friendship again."

Chrissy's phone vibrated. It was a new text from Gavin: *Hey. Hit me back when you get a chance. Kiss Grace 4 me.*

"It's Gavin. Let me call him back, Ma. Can you watch Grace for me? He and I may need to meet up face to face to discuss this New York move."

"That's fine, baby. I need to get all the time in with Grace as possible."

Chrissy went to the front room to return the call.

"Hey, Gavin, it's Chrissy. We need to talk."

"Okay, so talk."

Chrissy hated the way Gavin treated her sometimes. They had tried to become an item for the sake of Grace, but it was a no-go. He was definitely still in love with Faith, and it seemed that every time she tried to do right by him, he treated her worse because she *wasn't* Faith.

"We need to talk in person, Gavin."

"Fine, Chrissy. Meet me at the wing spot near Jackson State because I'm starving. I've been working at University Medical Center all day and I haven't had a chance to eat anything. Hey and be sure to bring my angel with you, too."

"It's late and I have already asked my mom to watch her while we talk." Chrissy heard Gavin suck his teeth. "But I'll go ahead and bring her. She hasn't seen you in two days and she's been calling for DA DA," Chrissy mocked baby Grace.

"See you in about 30 minutes then?" Gavin requested.

"Okay that's fine," Chrissy confirmed.

Her phone rang as soon as she hung up. She figured it was Gavin calling back, so she just flipped it open without looking at the Caller ID.

"Yes Gavin?" she said.

"Chrissy?" the female voice chimed.

Chrissy looked at the phone and saw the 415 area code. It was Faith. Before she could utter another word, the line went dead.

◅   ◅   ◅

Gavin couldn't fathom what Chrissy wanted to discuss. He hoped it wasn't about them trying to work on their relationship. That was a dead subject to him and required no further discussion. It wasn't that he didn't try to make it work with Chrissy, but getting her pregnant was an accident. Sleeping with her was even more of an accident. And he had lost his best friend and best girl in the process. Since everything had happened, he decided to leave alcohol alone. It had been the culprit to his relationship demise.

As much as he loved his baby Grace, he would have rather done it the right way with his wife...and his wife was supposed to be Faith.

He had replayed the events of last year over and over in his mind. Why was he so nice? Had he been a mean guy, he would have never offered to take Chrissy home from work when her brother didn't show up. If his mother hadn't called, he would have never had to ask Chrissy to wait on him to return her call before taking her home. If Remi hadn't been so gung ho to get home so he could go on a first date with Giselle, he wouldn't have stopped at his apartment to drop him off. If CSI hadn't been on with a new episode, they wouldn't have been in his room trying to watch it. If he didn't have that alcohol, they would have never drunk it. If, if, if. He always came to the conclusion that he would still be with Faith, IF.

He tried to call Faith, but she just didn't seem interested in talking to him. She never responded to his emails. He hoped that she got the flowers he sent. He read about her getting the big deal with Shay Praise online. He wanted her. He needed her. She was everything to him.

Just as he pulled into the wing spot, he got a call from his boy Remi.

"What up, man. It's been a whole minute, huh boy," Gavin answered happily.

"Yeah, bruh, it's been a while. Ya boy down here in Houston closing deals left and right. Between trying to be the next Donald Trump and being husband of the year, man, time just gets away from me. What you got up, G-Rob?"

"Dude, I can't call it...I'm still trying to get in med school. I am working at University Medical Center now, but I hope to hear something soon from all the schools I've applied to. You know applying to med school is a job in itself." He chuckled.

"I hear that, man. Well look, I just called you to see if you're going to be around for homecoming. I am making plans now to attend. I hope that Giselle and I will come to Jack-town with an extra care package, if you know what I mean."

"Oh snap, so y'all working on that parenting thing, huh. I hear you, dude. That's great, man. Good luck to y'all on that. I know you *putting it down*, so it's only a matter a time," Gavin teased his former college roommate. "Speaking of parenting, I am about to see my little angel real soon. Chrissy about to meet me up here at the wing spot near campus."

"Cool. How is Chrissy anyway? Y'all still trying to do that?"

"Naw dude, it didn't work out. We just co-parents now. That's all I can do with her, man. She's not Faith and that's pretty much who I want. So we stopped wasting our time. Just because you have a kid, doesn't make you automatically fall in love with your baby mamma. I love Grace and I respect Chrissy for being her mom, but I just can't do it, dawg. She's not the one for me."

"I hear you, man. It's funny y'all have a kid but no relationship and me and Giselle have a relationship with no kid. It's funny how things work out that way."

෯ ෯ ෯

Gavin ordered the wing special and took a seat at the nearest free table. Just as he bit into his first wing, Chrissy walked in toting Grace on her hip. "She looks just *like* me," he silently mouthed.

"Is that Daddy's angel coming?" Gavin greeted Grace. She returned the smile and hugged his neck tight. "Whoa, Daddy's girl is getting strong, huh. Give me a kiss, angel." Grace obliged and Gavin tickled her tummy.

"Hey, Chrissy, how you doing?"

"Great, Gavin. thanks for asking," she replied with a shocked look on her face. He was usually all about Grace and had recently seemed to zone out when it came to paying her any attention.

"You want something to eat? I can go up there and order you and Grace something."

"Thanks, but Grace just had spaghetti at Ma's house, and I am not hungry."

"All right, well you mind if I tear into these wings because a boy ain't ate all day."

"No, go right ahead." Chrissy watched Gavin tear into one wing after another. She thought about the night that Grace was conceived. Gavin had been eating wings that night, too. He and Remi had come up to Chili's where she was working to get some free food. She thought about that night. She had been such a fool to think that they would ever work out as a couple. He loved her friend Faith then, and he still did.

"Look Gavin, I am just going to cut to the chase. The vice president of marketing at All Black Designs has asked me to make a permanent move to New York and work in their Harlem office. I accepted and Grace and I will be moving in a month."

Gavin looked up from his plate with wing sauce on his mouth. "What? I thought you said you would be telecommuting for a while. A month, Chrissy? That's like right around the corner. I thought we would have time to discuss this so that we could decide what was best for Grace."

Grace looked at her daddy and smiled when he called her name. "DA DA," she said with a big smile.

"I know Gavin, but this is the opportunity of a lifetime and I already have everything worked out. The company has a daycare in the building and Grace will be there. She'll be close to me, so I won't have to worry about her. Plus I told you that I have two older cousins that live there. One is retired and the other one is married with kids, so I will have family up there supporting me."

"I don't know them," Gavin said with an attitude.

"You don't have to know them," Chrissy shot back. "They are *my* family. So that means they are Grace's family."

"This is just all of a sudden, Chrissy. I mean, I am trying to get into med school, you trying to take my baby from me and…"

"And what, Gavin? Huh? Am I supposed to wait to see where you land so that you can leave me and Grace? Oops I mean Grace, because you aren't leaving me. You've applied to all kinds of school all over the country, especially in California," she said with raised eyebrows, "and who knows where you will land. If you land near NYC, that would be ideal for Grace, but I can't be waiting on you. I'm moving forward with my life, Gavin. So it is what it is. Let's just make the best out of this, please."

"Fine, Chrissy…since you already have it all worked out, just give me my fatherly pecking orders so that I can know what I need to do," he replied sarcastically.

"Don't do that, Gavin. You know every decision that has ever been made about Grace has been made together. So this will be no different."

"All right whatever you say," he brushed her off and began playing with Grace.

"So you're going to move to the Big Apple on Daddy, huh, Angel. Daddy is sure going to miss you, but guess what, Daddy is going to make sure that he sees you at least once a month okay."

"Gavin, don't be telling her that. You know once you start med school, it's going to be hard to travel."

"I didn't say I would be the one traveling. You're going to bring her to me once a month if I can't make it up there."

"Oh really?" Chrissy laughed. "Boy, you have got some nerve. Some bold nerves at that."

"Look, I'll pay for y'all to come wherever I am, but like you said, my career might not allow me to travel so for the sake of Grace, we have to make this sacrifice."

"Sounds like I'm the one making the sacrifice, *Gavin.*"

"Only if I am unable to make it to see her, *Chrissy.*"

Both felt the tension in the air. Then it happened. Little Grace let one go and smiled. It was so loud, the couple in the next booth looked at them in disgust. Chrissy and Gavin both looked at each other and burst into laughter. Grace was their connection and that was all they had. They had to make the best of it. She didn't ask to be there, but she deserved the best they could offer her as parents.

"Look, Gavin, I agree that we have to make sacrifices for Grace. So here's the first one. I really need to go to NYC and get everything set up. Can you keep Grace for a little while, while I do that? Ma can watch her like she does now, when you have to work."

"Of course I can, Chrissy. This will be our bonding time before she leaves me." Gavin stared at his daughter. It was like looking into a mirror. She had his light brown skin. She didn't get any of her looks from Chrissy who was considered fair skinned. Chrissy and Gavin did have one thing in common and that was jet black hair. All three shared that trait.

"Great! I will make plans to return in October. I'll just come back for the wedding and homecoming and then take Grace up to New York after that."

"Wait, what wedding?"

"Oh, yeah I forgot to tell you, Faith's aunt Jackie and Darnell are getting married. And the wedding is that Friday night during Jackson

State's homecoming weekend. She told me at church Sunday to extend you an invite."

Gavin's mind began to race. He knew Faith would be coming home for that. Excitement began to overtake him. This would be his time to get her back.

Chrissy knew what Gavin was thinking by the dreamy expression on his face. She shook her head and smiled.

Chapter 5

Journal Entry #2

*Why would she do that? Why would she answer the phone and say
his name? I'm over him or am I? Why I am so fuming mad because she
mentioned his name. I've forgiven them. I really have. But I just can't
quite forget it. No matter what I do. Sometimes I let my mind go all the
way back to the day that I walked in on them. I need to stop rehashing
the past and just move forward. That's a lot easier said or in this case
written, than actually doing. I need a real person to talk to. No offense,
Journal, but I need a voice to come back at me.*

"Chrishawn, it's Faith. I need to talk."

"Hey, girl, what's going on? What's the deal?"

"I just called Chrissy and she answered the phone as if I was
Gavin. I know I am overreacting, but it just made me so mad that she
would do that. Who doesn't look at their phone before they answer
it?"

"Chrissy," Chrishawn replied. "That girl never looks at her phone
because every time I call her, instead of greeting me with hey big
brother, she says hello like she doesn't know my number. So I am
pretty sure it was an error on her part. I've told you before that Chrissy
wants to be friends with you, like y'all used to be."

"I know, but I just don't desire that friendship anymore. Plus I'm
here and she's there. Hey speaking of...her number has a New York
area code. What's up with that?" Faith asked.

"Well she has a new gig and they are based in New York, but she
telecommutes, so she doesn't have to actually be in New York, but the
phone they provided her is a New York number."

"Oh okay. So who does she work for and what is she doing now?"

"Baby girl, now you know how I feel about this. We decided together that we would not discuss stuff you and Chrissy should discuss. Those are the rules we put in place, remember?"

"Umm hmm, yeah I remember," Faith reluctantly replied.

"Okay then, so what else is up? Did you enjoy your party?"

"Yeah, it was cool. I was kind of glad that it didn't last a long time. Don't get me wrong, I enjoyed celebrating with you and the co-workers, but I see them all day everyday. It was cool to have a little happy hour type function here though, especially on Elite's dime. I didn't get a chance to ask you about your day while you were over here. Then you rushed out of here with everybody else."

"Well I didn't want people to see me staying afterwards because then they would have felt they could stay longer, too. Plus I needed to get back home to finish up this itinerary for tomorrow's youth trip. You know we're taking the youth to Alacatraz for a tour."

"Yeah, that's right. I wish I could go, but I need to run some errands tomorrow. Plus I just found out my aunt is getting married."

"What? Jackie is getting married? To Darnell?"

"Yes and yes. The wedding is going to be during Jackson State's homecoming weekend. So I have to go and try on a dress at Nordstrom tomorrow because guess who's in it…ya girl."

"So how do you feel about that?" Chrishawn asked.

"Well, at first I was like, oh no, I'm not ready to deal with this now. But after some serious prayer, I think I am ready. Things will be weird, but weird ain't always bad."

"With God, Faith, anything is possible, including learning how to deal with two sets of parents."

"Yeah, I know. Are you planning on coming home that weekend, too?"

"I am going to try. But my schedule at the church is super busy. Being youth director ain't no joke. But I take it all in stride because I could be back in Jackson doing nothing with my life. So I am thankful to God for the opportunity."

"I need to get my flight and arrange to leave earlier than I thought since the wedding is on the Friday before the homecoming game that Saturday. I wonder if my aunt will have a bachelorette party." Faith laughed. "Knowing Aunt J, she got it all planned out."

Chrishawn's line beeped.

"Hey, Faith, this is actually my sister on the other line. Let me holler at her and then call you back."

"Oh…okay," Faith stuttered. "Would you tell her that I will call her later."

"How about we stick to the rules and you just call her on your own without my input."

"You make me sick…bye, Shawny."

"Love you, too, baby girl." He laughed before clicking over. "Hello?"

"Hey, big brother. How's the big time youth director doing?" Chrissy teased.

"Hey, sis, I'm doing good. Staying busy with the church of course. And what about you and my beautiful niece?

"We're both good. She's just growing up so fast. I can't believe how big she is."

"Well can a brother get a recent picture or something? I still got the one from when she was playing on the swing at the park with Momma."

"Oh yeah, she was too cute and looked so grown on that picture. How about I take one when we hang up and send it to your phone? She still looks just like her daddy though. That hasn't changed," Chrissy emphasized.

"Let's not go down that road, Chris. We already know she looks like Gavin. You don't have to dwell on that. She's still a beautiful baby and you should thank God for a healthy baby girl. Forget about Gavin. Well, I mean that *is* her daddy, but forget about the drama with him and just be co-parents to her. At this point in your life, you just need to move on and get yours."

"Funny you should say that…that's why I'm calling. Your little sister is moving to New York!"

"Whoa, wait a minute. New York? I thought you were just working in Jackson for a company *in* New York.."

"The opportunity has come, and I am moving, Chrishawn. Me and Grace are moving."

"How are you going to take care of Grace and…"

"Slow your roll, big brother. I got it all figured out. Plus you know we got family there, too."

"Oh that's right, I forgot about that. I'm the one all alone here on the West coast with no family. All I got is my girl Faith."

"Yeah," Chrissy said dryly.

"Don't be that way, Chrissy. Me and Faith are doing good here in Cali, and like I've told you *and her* before…I don't mix friends and family spats. So whatever you want to say, save it for when you talk to her."

"I wasn't going to say anything, other than the fact that she called me and then hung up on me."

"Yeah I heard about that. Look, y'all two will get it together eventually. Just because I am the common denominator, don't keep trying to make me the mediator," he pressed. "Now back to this stuff about you moving to NYC with my niece. When is this all going down?"

"Next month, but I am planning to go next week to get everything together. Grace will be staying with Gavin while I am gone. Of course Momma will probably be watching her the majority of the time because of his crazy work schedule. But I will be back the weekend of Jackson

State's homecoming for Jackie and Darnell's wedding and of course I can't miss the homecoming game. You still coming home?"

"I don't know. I was just telling Faith that I am working like a Hebrew slave. Okay, I shouldn't say that. But anyway, I got a lot going on so I don't know if I will make it home. I know I am coming for Thanksgiving though. Will you and Grace be back home then?"

"Oh yeah, for sure. I can't see myself spending Thanksgiving in the N-Y-C. I'm too country for that. I'm going to need my greens, chitterlings, ham hocks and smoked turkey necks."

"You can always just go to Sylvia's. Isn't that a soul food restaurant there?"

"Yeah, well, whatever. I'm going to be right at Charnese's Place."

They both laughed.

"All right then, well keep me posted, girl. We don't talk enough as it is and now that you moving from home, it's probably going to be harder."

"I'll make sure we keep in touch and send pictures. Just think, little Grace is going to be raised up as a city girl." Chrissy chuckled. "She'll be sounding so proper when she comes back to Mississippi to visit." Chrissy thought deeply about her baby. She never really imagined her daughter not being raised in the south.

"Well, just don't let her ever forget where she really comes from. She ain't no more a New Yorker than I am a Californian. We from the Sip, all day, every day, sis!"

"I know. Don't remind me."

"All right girl, you better not get up there and act all citified either. You's a country gal, ya hear me," he replied in the most country tone he could muster.

"Talk to you later Chrishawn."

"All right, Chris. Hey don't forget to call Faith."

"Thought you weren't mixing friends and family?"

"I'm not. Just call her. I know she'll be happy for you and the new adventure you're about to take. Love you, sis."

"Love you, too, big brother."

Chrissy thought about it and before she could change her mind, she dialed Faith's phone. It was time to talk.

Chapter 6

It had been a long day and Giselle was happy to be spending the evening with her honey. She pulled into the long driveway that led to their brick two-story home. She admired the freshly manicured lawn. *Alfredo Luiz has been here.*

She remembered when Remi surprised her with the home. It was like a dream come true. She knew when Remi decided to work at his father's real estate firm they would eventually get a house, but she never imagined one so palatial. The laguna pool in the back always made her feel like she was living *high on the hog*, as her folks back home would say. She recognized how blessed they were, but having a baby was really starting to weigh on her faith. Quickly losing her homeowner excitement, she pressed the button in her red Ford Flex and the garage door began to open. She looked around before pulling in. She had a habit of making sure no one was around when she pulled in. Lately, there had been too many news reports of driveway abductions.

I wonder what time Remi is coming home.

She walked through the back door which led directly to the kitchen and there they were staring her directly in the face, a dozen red and white roses. *He is the sweetest man.* She rushed over to take a whiff. The aroma engulfed her senses and instantly took away her self doubt. At that moment, she felt like the most blessed woman in the world. How could she doubt God? Not when He had already given her so much.

She wondered when Remi had time to come home and bring her roses. She dialed his office number.

"Remi Aguilar speaking."

"Hey baby, you are so sweet! Thank you so much for making my day with these beautiful flowers. They are just absolutely gorgeous."

"Flowers…what flowers are you talking about?" he asked with a serious tone.

"Remi, stop playing. The roses you left for me on the kitchen island."

"I didn't leave any roses for you on the kitchen island, Giselle. I have been swamped at work all day. I barely had enough time to eat, so be ready when I get home because I am starving. I can't wait to try that new spot."

"Wait a minute, Remi. If you didn't get me the flowers, then who did?"

"I don't know, G. Is there a card with the flowers?"

Giselle went back in the kitchen to search through the flowers. She had been removing her work clothes in their master suite.

"Let me go look. I just assumed they were from you when I walked in. I mean who else has a key to our home."

"My parents do. And then there's…"

"Hold on, Remi. I am getting the card out now. We'll just see who they are from. Remi, this is crazy. I don't want anybody just coming up in our house all willy nilly like that. I love your parents and all, but…"

Giselle stopped her ranting mid-sentence.

"See you play too much," she shouted at the phone.

Remi began laughing so hard that he almost fell out of his office chair.

"Now, baby, you know good and well ain't nobody been in our house. I can't believe you fell for that one." He continued laughing.

"You just get on home, Mr. Aguilar. You want to play games, huh. Well I got more where that comes from. Watch yourself because you are certainly due for a thrashing." She smiled.

"Giselle, I already hid the super soaker water gun, so don't even think about retaliation."

"Oh don't you worry about anything, my dear heart. Just keep your eyes open at all times."

"Honey, you're scaring me," he teased.

"You better be," she retorted.

Remi and Giselle hung up and Giselle admired her roses again. Just as she was about to return to getting out of her work clothes, their home phone rang.

"Hello."

"Is ah a Mr. Aguilar there?" the female voice sang.

"No he's not, who may I ask is calling? This is his wife."

"Umph, his *wife* huh?" the voice replied.

Giselle's eyebrows quickly rose. "Who is this?"

"Can you tell Mr. Aguilar that an old friend called?"

"Well old friend, what is your name?"

"Well, WIFE, I don't think that is any of your business since I am calling for MISTER Aguilar. Thank you though. I will call back when I see his truck pull in."

Then the call went dead. Giselle just stood there staring at the phone. She thought about calling Remi back, but decided to call the number back instead. She wasn't about to be punked in her own house by some old female friend of Remi's. And what did she mean when she *sees* his truck pull in. She ran to the bay window in the front room and peered out the window. Now that he was back in town and doing well, the *old friends* were bound to come looking. But she had a surprise for them. Remi was married to her and try they might, nothing was going to come between their love.

She dialed the number and waited for the person to pick up. The phone went to a voicemail. *Perfect, I can listen to the outgoing message.*

"This is the day that the Lord has made and I am glad in it. You've reached my voicemail. Please leave a message and I will return your call when I can. Thanks and have a blessed day in the Lord."

What in the world? Who was this old friend? She definitely has a split personality. Just as the phone beeped for Giselle to leave a message, she hung up. *What kind of message could I leave after hearing something like that?*

Giselle decided not to let the strange call ruin her night. She went back to the master suite to select her outfit for the night. They were going to the new Brazilian restaurant, so she wanted to look cute for her hubby. She selected a black halter dress that flared at the waist. Her black diamond Aldo sandals would match perfectly. She went into the bathroom to shower and change her toe nail polish. Remi loved when she surprised him with a new color. He was a feet man and she made sure she kept her feet up to par just for him.

About 45 minutes later, she heard Remi's blue hummer pull up. She looked out the window and saw her man getting out of the advertised laden truck. It had been his idea to put the real estate company's info all over the truck with screen prints. They couldn't go anywhere without Remi advertising what business he was in. It felt like they were riding around in a mobile billboard. Remi loved it.

And as much as she liked for him to get new business, Giselle didn't particularly like her husband's cell number plastered all over his truck. But she trusted him and that was all that really mattered. She quickly donned her red silk robe and rushed to meet Remi at the door.

"WOW, girl. You look scrumptious. We may need to just stay in tonight."

"Funny. Minutes ago you were sooo hungry."

Remi admired the smoothness of Giselle's neckline accented by the silky red robe she wore.

"I'm looking at dinner so what's *your* point?"

Giselle pranced around the counter to give Remi his welcome home hug and kiss. She held him tightly and inhaled his cologne. *I love this man.*

"My point is this," she said and seductively kissed him. She was so glad they were married and could now be intimate without feeling guilty. It had been hard trying to convince Remi to be celibate at first, but they had managed to pull it off. Remi had reminded her time and time again how proud he was that their relationship had been pure until their wedding night. It made their union even more special.

"Okay, girl, you're going to get something started."

"You right, we can get it started *after* we eat." She laughed. "I'm really hungry and I can't wait to try out this new place. Will you be ready soon?"

"Yeah, I just need to shower real quick, and then we can be out."

Remi dashed off to the master bath and started the shower.

∾ ∾ ∾

"I have a delivery here ma'am from a Mister...."

"Yeah, yeah, yeah, I know who it's from. Just give me the thing so I can electronically sign for it."

"Okay, ma'am. I see you are in a rush, so here you go."

Jacob was new on the job and today was his first day delivering packages by himself. Not your average muscle man delivery guy, Jacob's skinny frame and nerdy black square glasses usually made people think they could run him over. He was working on becoming more assertive, but this woman, as beautiful as she was, scared the mess out of him.

"There it's signed, now give me my package."

"Sure Miss…"

"Do you struggle to read everybody's name? Just give me my package and be out, brother."

Jacob looked stunned, but then quickly handed over the sealed letter-size package. "Yes, ma'am. You have a nice day." He smiled and gritted his teeth. The ventriloquist in him added, "If that's possible."

Before he could utter another word, the door was slammed. *Man, I hope all my deliveries on Ashby Lane aren't this rude. This is supposed to be a really nice neighborhood. I guess I assumed the people would be nice too. Oh well, next stop.*

Back inside the house, the sealed envelope was ripped open.

Finally...the check. Let me see if he kept his word and made it out to the school. Dang. He did. Oh well, I will get Lavisha at the school to cash it and give me the money. She'll do it for a little extra change on the side. Ha! Mr. Aguilar doesn't know who he's dealing with. I am a smart and savvy business woman. I wouldn't be living in this posh home for free if I wasn't. Nobody screws me and gets away with it. Nobody!

∽ ∽ ∽

"Baby, you ready to ride?" Remi called out.

"I sure am." Giselle beamed as she came down the spiral staircase. "Let's take the Flex."

"Awe, come on baby. You know I like to advertise my business as much as possible. Let's take the hummer. Who knows, a million dollar deal may need me to close it, and it won't know it needs me until my truck passes it by." He chuckled. "You know God intervention...right time and right place?"

Giselle rolled her eyes. *I got a deal you need to close and I need some God intervention. Right time, right place is exactly what I am thinking...but for this baby, not for your real estate business.*

"Remi, seriously, you already are working 24/7, and you know every time we go anywhere in the hummer, people just call you because they see your number plastered all over the truck. Honey, please. Today has been trying enough. After the news from the nurse and my rude new co-worker, I just want to hang with my honey and enjoy the night in peace. Can you give me that, baby?"

"Okay, G. But I want to hear more about this rude new co-worker of yours. How can anybody be rude to my baby? You are the sweetest, most beautiful, kindest, brown sugar in the world."

Giselle smiled. "Come on, suck up, let's ride out. I'll even let you drive the Flex."

"What? I can't believe it. You're letting *me*, mister heavy feet, drive the Flex? Let's dip before you change your mind."

Just as Remi set the house alarm and was about to go out the door, the phone rang. "Darn, let me grab that."

He rushed over to the cordless phone on the black granite kitchen counter and picked up panting.

"Yeah, hello?"

"Remi Aguilar?"

"Yeah, this is he."

"Hey, this is your old high school buddy ReRe. I heard you were back in town. How is everything going with you?"

"ReRe! Hey, girl. Everything is going good. I haven't talked to you since spring..." He stopped himself mid-sentence, not wanting to bring up freshman year spring break. "How you doing girl?" He beamed.

"I'm good, Remi. I saw our classmate Sharon the other day and she told me that you were back in town working for your father's real estate firm. She actually said y'all saw each other while stuck in traffic on I-10."

"Yep, sure did. I was in my new hummer and I got our homeboy from high school Shakile to hook it up with some tight screen-print graphics to advertise the business. You remember big Shakile from band? Yeah, he hooked it up right, too. Anyway, that's how Sharon noticed me. I get all kind of attention and new business calls with that truck. I am trying to convince my dad to get a hummer, too, but he says that's for the young folks to be riding around in stuff like that."

ReRe and Remi shared a laugh and Remi was just about to get into another topic before he heard Giselle clear her throat behind him. She had come in to turn the alarm off before the cops rolled up.

Remi turned around and she bucked her eyes as if to say, would you come on here.

"ReRe, look, I am so glad you called. We'll have to catch up real soon. How did you get my number anyway?"

"I Googled it, boy. You know you can find anything on Google." She laughed.

"Yeah, that's what's up. Look, my wife is waiting because we are about to go and try out that new Brazilian spot. How about I call you later and we can catch up. Maybe you can come by the house and meet my wife. We are going to do a barbeque for Labor Day and I was going to invite a few people over that I've reconnected with since I've been home."

"That sounds like a plan, Remi. I'm not married yet, but I'd love to bring my boyfriend over if that's cool."

"Yeah, that's no problem. I'll give you a call with all the details. As a matter of fact, just shoot me an email with your info." He gave her his e-mail address.

"Okay got it. Talk to you later, Remi. Tell your wife hello and I can't wait to meet her. Not sure who would want to marry your crazy self, so I need to see her in person."

"Very funny, Re. I'll holla at you later, girl."

Remi disconnected the call.

"So who was that?" Giselle pried.

"That was one of my homegirls from high school. We were in the band together and we used to kick it all the time. We lived on the same block and her folks and my folks were real cool back in the day. When the grown folks would get together, us kids would hang out. We kept in touch for a little bit while I was at JSU, but band always kept me so busy. Then she kind of stopped emailing me. I figured life just took over, so I didn't press it. It was cool to hear from her though."

Remi knew he wasn't telling Giselle the whole truth about his past with ReRe, but it was the past and he had moved forward since then. But it didn't keep him from thinking about his last encounter with ReRe. She had been one of the prettiest girls at his high school. They had always been good friends and neighbors. He wanted more from her and always tried to get at her, but she never wanted to ruin their friendship with sex, that was until he came home from JSU for spring break his freshman year. For some reason, ReRe had changed her mind since high school.

Remi thought back to that day. He remembered how ReRe was like a whole new person. She still looked good, but her personality had changed so much since high school. Remi remembered how she was literally ready to throw herself on him when they saw each other at the mall.

      ◌   ◌   ◌

"ReRe is that you girl?"

"Oh, um yeah. What's up, baby? How you been doing?

Baby? Wow, she's changed a lot since she started college.

"I've been fine. You know I'm at JSU playing in the Sonic Boom now."

"Oh yeah, that's what's up."

"How your folks been? I've only been home a few days, but I have been meaning to come over and holla at y'all."

"Everybody's cool. Look, I'm on my way to pick up an outfit for the big party at the Roxy tonight. You gone be there?"

"Oh yeah, for sho. I didn't know you did the club thing."

Remi noticed how fine ReRe was looking in her tight jeans and tight Baby Phat graphic print tee. She was definitely still fine as the day they graduated from Jack Yates High School.

"There's a lot you don't know about me," she flirted.

Remi felt himself getting excited at her advances.

That night Remi and ReRe took Tequila shots and danced the night away on the dance floor at Club Roxy. Both had been dancing so hot and heavy that when Remi suggested they leave, ReRe gladly followed him out the club. They didn't even wait to get out of the club parking lot before they started aggressively kissing each other. Not wanting to miss the moment to hit that, Remi and ReRe got into the back seat of Remi's father's Cadillac Escalade and made it happen. He had finally conquered the finest girl from his high school.

After they finished, she kissed Remi and decided to go back into the club and ride home with her friends. Remi left the club and that was the last he had heard of ReRe. When she didn't email him, he figured their little sexual encounter had put a blemish on their friendship. He was headed back to JSU in a few days anyway, so he just left it alone. They were worlds apart with him being in Mississippi and her being in Houston.

◈   ◈   ◈

"So I heard you invited her to the BBQ. That was nice. It'll be fun to meet some of your old friends. I can't wait to hear some of the stories about when you were in high school. I bet you were a trip."

"Baby, I was very popular in high school. All the girls wanted them some Remi," he teased.

"Yeah right…just like all the girls at J-State wanted you, too. Gavin already told me how you like to over exaggerate stuff. But all that matters now is I got you."

"And I got you, girl." Remi embraced and kissed Giselle, then the two left for the restaurant.

In the car Giselle wondered if this ReRe girl was the same one who had called earlier and been so rude. *We'll just see who we are dealing with when she comes by the house. I won't make any assumptions right now.*

Remi was hoping that inviting ReRe over to his house wasn't going to start any old flame feelings. Their little encounter had only been a quickie and it had never been brought up again. Plus, she was bringing her man over anyway.

Chapter 7

Faith saw her cell phone ringing last night. But she wasn't ready to talk to Chrissy. *I'll talk to her later,* she concluded before going to bed last night.

She grabbed her iPod and headed out. It was early Saturday morning, and the sun was beaming down on the hilly streets of San Francisco. Faith was ready to get her exercise on. Her white tennis shoes were laced and her ponytail was intact. Instead of going to the gym, she decided to walk the city. Her normal routine on Saturday included exercise and a nice breakfast at Mama's On Washington Square, a popular breakfast place in North Beach. Malik had taken her there her first weekend in San Francisco.

Being from Mississippi, she doubted anybody could replicate the type of southern breakfast she was used to, but Mama's, on the corner of Stockton and Filbert, gave her a new type of home-cooked flavor to savor.

Just as she rounded the corner on Stockton, Faith felt her phone vibrating in her pocket. *Great, now who could this be? It's too early for anybody to be calling me.* She retrieved her phone from her jacket pocket. It was Aunt Jackie. She decided to pick up.

"Hey, Aunt Jackie, what's up?"

"Hey, hot pocket. What are you doing out this early?" Jackie could hear the wind blowing from Faith's phone. The breeze from the Bay was coming through.

"Oh, I'm just out for my morning walk, that's all. What are you doing?"

"I'm going through my wedding checklist. Have you been to get your dress yet? I need to mark that off my list."

"It's on my list to do today. Don't worry, Aunt Jackie. I'll take care of it."

"Okay, honey. I just got so much going on and Darnell ain't helping me with nothing. You know how men are, child. They just want their to-do list, not all the details." She laughed.

Faith could tell her aunt was so excited about getting married. She truly was happy for her. It was funny that her real parents were actually getting married. She hadn't taken the time to digest the thought too much since finding out, but the more she thought about it, she realized how much of a blessing it was.

"Well, is there anything I can help you with? I mean, from here?"

"No, baby, I got it all together. I just want to make sure everything goes well. I wish you were here sometimes, Faith, but I know you're a grown woman now living in San Francisco and you got your own life to live. And speaking of, how is your love life. You and Chrishawn hanging in there?"

"We sure are. He's been awesome since I moved here. We're just taking it one day at a time though. We don't want to push things too fast, you know. So I wouldn't really call it a love life. We're just really good friends and we'll see what happens."

Faith heard her aunt suck her teeth. She knew what that meant.

"Yeah, okay, we'll see what happens. I hope you are not still hung up over Gavin. That's your past, baby."

That's what the teeth sucking meant. She knew her aunt was about to go down that road and she had pulled right on up to Gavin Drive.

"Aunt Jackie, I *am* getting over Gavin. But he sent me flowers the other day congratulating me on getting the new account."

"How did he even know about that?"

Faith noticed the long line at Mama's. She needed to go ahead and get in line.

"I don't know. He's probably been keeping up with my career I'm sure. You know he's bent on getting me back. But I'm really done. I wish he would just focus on his child and Chrissy."

"Well, I don't know about Chrissy, but he definitely needs to be focused on his child. Have you talked to Chrissy yet?"

"No. She called me last night, but I wasn't ready yet. I need to get myself together first."

"What is there to get together, Faith? Why you are avoiding Chrissy like the plague? Just talk to her. She's going to be at the wedding when you come home. And you are dating her brother for goodness' sake. You have to let the past go, Faith," she nearly screamed.

Faith didn't know how to respond to her aunt. She felt herself tearing up. The tears started rolling. She knew she needed to finally let it go, but for some reason she kept holding it. Her aunt was more than right. But while she forgave Chrissy, it was hard to forget.

As if her aunt was reading her silence, she quietly spoke.

"Faith, you have to stop looking back and move forward, honey. God makes all things new. He will give you the strength, but you have to trust Him."

The tears were coming so fast that Faith stepped out of the line at Mama's and walked over to Washington Square Park. She took a seat on the park bench and continued crying in silence. *Why is it so hard to forget and move forward? Every time I think I've moved on, it comes back to me even harder than the last time I remembered it.*

"But I loved him, Aunt Jackie. I really did love Gavin." There she finally said it. It had been brewing in her mind and spirit like a pot of coffee since she left Mississippi. Her work and Chrishawn would temporarily take the steam off the brew, but it was still there.

"I know, honey, but he's not what God wants for you."

"How do I know that for sure, Aunt Jackie? What if I was supposed to have helped Gavin? You know…stuck by his side and helped him become a better man in Christ?"

Faith continued to cry and ignored the homeless man who sat down beside her on the park bench.

"Faith, you listen to me. If you were meant to do that, God wouldn't have moved you away from Gavin. I know you loved him and cared for him, and I am sure you did help him become a better man in Christ through your Christ-like actions. But it's over with him, Faith. You know that in your heart it's really over, but you don't want to let it go. You've got a nice young man there in San Fran who's there for you and you're missing out on his greatness because you are still living and hanging on to your past."

Just as her aunt was about to go on, Faith's phone beeped. She had another call coming in. She peered at the phone and it was Chrishawn calling her. She laughed to herself.

"Aunt Jackie, this is Chrishawn calling me now. Can I call you back?"

"Sure, honey. Call me later and stop that crying in public. You know how crazy your face looks when you cry." She chuckled.

Faith couldn't help but laugh. She hated the way she looked when she cried. She definitely didn't have a cute girl cry.

She hung up from Aunt Jackie and clicked over, but Chrishawn had already gone to voicemail. *Shoot I missed him.*

"I missed him, too," said the voice next to her on the bench. Faith was briefly startled, but then smiled at the homeless man.

"How did you miss him?" the man asked. Faith didn't know what he was talking about.

"Excuse me, sir, I was talking about a missed call. Who did you miss?" she asked with a look of confusion as the man wrestled with the plastic grocery bags. They appeared to have shoes and additional clothing in them. It was probably all he owned, Faith surmised.

"I missed when Jesus came by with some food," he replied with his head down.

Not really sure how to respond, Faith looked at the older black man in front of her. He looked like he was in his sixties and his salt and pepper beard hadn't had a haircut *since* the sixties. He wreaked something awful and had on a trench coat that probably hadn't been washed since he owned it. Her heart felt for him.

She decided to pry a little more into his Jesus story. "So when did Jesus come by with food?"

"Earlier, but I missed him. Did you see Him?"

"I must have missed Him too since I was on the phone," she played along.

"Yeah, I saw you on the phone and I figured you missed Him too because you were crying."

Faith laughed to herself. "Well, what time does He come back?"

"Oh He'll be back. He always comes right on time. You see, I'm hungry, but I can wait on Him to come back."

Faith looked over at Mama's and noticed the line had gone down tremendously. She had never done anything like this before, but she felt God pulling at her.

"Well, I was just getting ready to go over to Mama's and get some breakfast, you want to join me?"

For the first time, the man gave her eye contact. He had the most beautiful hazel eyes and his smile could warm up any room he stepped foot in. *I bet once he gets cleaned up, he's a handsome old guy.*

"That's mighty nice of you, young lady. Sometimes Jesus sends His angels to feed me and you must be one of them."

Faith got up from the bench and watched as the homeless man gathered his bags.

"So what's your name, sir?"

"Gavin. Gavin Roberts."

Faith stopped dead in her tracks. The moment felt surreal. Like she had been in this spot before. Then she remembered when she met her biological father for the first time. When he said his name, she fainted. It was that feeling all over again. "I'm sorry, what did you say your name was?"

"Gavin," the man replied, mirroring the same weird face Faith was giving him. He was ready to continue the stroll across the street to the restaurant when Faith looked at him up and down. "Is there something wrong, young lady?"

"Um, well, yeah," Faith stuttered to figure out what to say next. This couldn't be *her* Gavin's father, or would it be his grandfather? Faith wracked her brain, but couldn't remember whether Gavin was a junior or third or first.

"Sir, this may sound weird, but my boyfriend, I mean ex-boyfriend," Faith shook her head and quickly corrected herself. "He has the exact same name. Are you from San Francisco?"

"No lil lady, but I've been here for years. I'm originally from Atlanta. I do have a son and a grandson with the same name though. Tell me about your boyfriend. I mean ex-boyfriend," he quickly corrected himself as she had done.

"Well he's from Atlanta," Faith exclaimed. "And his mother's name is Sheryl and he has a sister name Gavanna. And…"

The homeless man began to laugh. His was laughing so hard that he began to cough a deep cough. One of those coughs that made your chest hurt.

"Sir, what is so funny? Are you okay?"

He kept laughing while trying to catch his breath and clear his throat. "Now ain't this something. Of all the people I could have met today, Jesus, I've met my grandson's girlfriend. I mean ex-girlfriend. You got me this time, Lord." He kept laughing.

Faith couldn't believe it. Was this really Gavin's grandfather? Here in San Francisco? This homeless man?

Before she could catch herself, she dialed his number from memory.

"Hello," Gavin answered.

She held the phone. She hadn't talked to him since she left a year ago.

"Faith is that you?" Gavin asked while beaming on the other end of the phone. He couldn't believe it was her. His prayers had been answered. His dreams had come true. She was calling him. He pictured what she looked like. All he could muster up in his memory was how she looked the last time he saw her. They were at the church for his daughter's baby dedication ceremony and she was dressed in one of her signature business suits, looking fine as ever. *Thank you God.*

"Hi, Gavin. Yes it's me. Are you busy right now?"

Gavin had been knocked out on his couch. After meeting with Chrissy about her move, he had come home and crashed for the night.

"Oh no, I'm not busy," he quickly responded. He sat up on the couch and cleared the groggy morning sound from his throat. "How are you, Faith? I've missed you so much, girl. I am so happy you called me."

"Gavin, slow your roll. I'm not really calling to chit chat with you this early, okay." She wiped the sweat beads that were now forming at her hairline. This conversation had to be quick, otherwise she would get caught up – and getting caught up on the phone with Gavin was the last thing she needed to do. Wanted to do, maybe, but definitely didn't need to do.

"Gavin, look. I am here in the park and I just met a man who has your same name. He says he is your grandfather," she stated. The homeless man was continuing to walk ahead of her toward Mama's. Clearly he was too hungry to deal with Faith questioning his identity. He looked back at her talking to Gavin and laughed to himself. "I know who I am lil lady, but more importantly I know *whose* I am," he mumbled more to himself than to Faith.

"My grandfather?" Gavin said. "Are you serious?"

Faith noticed the elder Gavin continuing his stride and rushed to catch up with him. "Hold up, Mr. Roberts, I have your grandson on the phone now. Do you want to speak with him?"

Gavin couldn't believe what he was hearing. This is not how he imagined his first reconnection conversation with Faith to go. "Faith, wait. I don't know if I want to talk to him. I mean I don't really know this man. I know that I have his name, but I don't know him like that."

"Well, Gavin, he's apparently your grandfather and he's right here in my face. What do you want me to do? I mean, I just met him here in the park." Then she lowered her voice. "Gavin, he's homeless."

"What," he screamed. "No Faith, you have got to be lying to me. My grandfather, homeless?"

"I'm not kidding, Gavin. Do you want to speak with him?"

Gavin got up from the couch. He was now pacing around his apartment. *My grandfather is homeless?* He couldn't believe it. He didn't have a relationship with his grandfather at all, nor his father for that matter, but to know that someone in his family was homeless did something to him.

"Gavin, are you still there?"

"I'm here," he stuttered. "Faith, I don't think I want to talk to him. We know of each other, but I don't know him. But I am concerned that he is homeless. I'm going to call my mother right now. I need to find my father and speak with him. I need to talk to somebody else in my family right now because this is too much. It's overwhelming, Faith."

Faith could hear the worry in Gavin's voice. She felt for him. She questioned whether or not she should have called him. She asked God to guide her, and then she spoke. "I understand, Gavin. Here's what I am going to do. I'm going to go ahead and take him over to Mama's restaurant like we were headed before I called you, and get him something to eat. Then I am going to put him up in a hotel. Once you talk to your mother, call me back and we'll go from there, okay?"

"Okay, baby. Thank you so much, Faith. I love you."

"Gavin, let's not okay. Just give me a call once you talk to your folks." And with that, Faith thumbed the end button on her cell phone.

"Everything okay with you, young lady?" the elder Roberts asked as they got their place in the short line. People were staring at Mr. Roberts, and Faith could see the frowns on their faces for him being in line near them.

"Yes, sir. Gavin is going to call his mom so that he can reach your son. Everything will be okay now, Mr. Roberts." She nervously smiled.

"Why would he do that?" he asked. "I know how to reach my son. The thing is my son doesn't want anything to do with me. So I let him be."

"But does he know you are homeless?" Faith asked, worried. *How could anyone know their dad is homeless and not want to come and rescue them?*

"Yes, he knows. But his heart is hard, and he doesn't care about me. We've been estranged for more years than I wish to remember, but it's okay though, I have my faith and that is what gets me through each day. I have never begged for bread nor have I been forsaken. My God takes care of me. I may be homeless and living in a shelter, but as you young folks say, it's all good." He laughed.

"How long have you been homeless and how did this happen?"

"Well I lost my job and couldn't find another one, then I started missing payments on the house and it got foreclosed on. I rented a place for a little while, but when my unemployment ran out, I had to leave that place. I've been trying to find another job for the last two years, but the economy hasn't really helped. There are more and more people coming to the shelter everyday because of lost jobs. I admit, I was living paycheck to paycheck and wasn't really saving any money for a rainy day."

"And what about your other family?"

"I knew I had a grandson, but my son is an only child and his mother and I weren't together long after he was born. So when Junior and I fell out over some money, our relationship pretty much vanished. He did call me and tell me about lil Gavin, but that was it.

"He said he wanted me to know there was another Gavin Roberts in the world and he would do his best to make sure he was more like him than me. Those were his exact words. It stung of course, because I only wanted the best for my son. He just didn't want the best for himself."

"Yeah, Gavin didn't grow up with his father or I would have known that. But I didn't know he was a third."

"Well he's not. His middle name is different from mine and Junior's. Our middle name is Lee and I believe Lil Gavin's middle name is Tremaine or Jermaine or something like that."

"It's Tremaine," Faith said. Of course she knew his name; he had been the love of her life.

As they made their way into the restaurant, Faith and the elder Gavin ordered and found themselves a seat at the back of the restaurant. Many of the patrons were staring at them like they had never seen a person reach out and feed the homeless before. Maybe they hadn't.

"Well I told Gavin that I'm not allowing you to stay on the streets any longer. You're going to a hotel and I am paying for it."

"Now I can't let you do that, young lady. You keep your money. This food here is all I need."

"Oh no, sir." She waved her hand while swallowing the last of her home fries. "You're going to take my hotel offer and that's final. I love Gavin and you're his grandfather, so there's no need to fight me on this one okay." *What did I just say? I love Gavin?*

Before she knew it, the elder Gavin had zeroed in on her last statement. "Whoa, wait a minute. I thought you said he was your *ex*-boyfriend?"

"Look, Mr. Roberts, it's complicated…me and Gavin, but I do care for him and I can't go back to my place knowing that you are homeless. That's just unacceptable and not how we do things in Mississippi. We take care of people, even if we don't half know them."

"Mississippi? You're from Mississippi? I assumed you were from Atlanta. How did you and Gavin meet?" he asked.

"Gavin and I both attended Jackson State University. We met my freshman year in band camp. I was a majorette and he played drums."

"My grandson plays the drums," he exclaimed with lifted eyebrows. "Wow, that's awesome. I played the drums, too!"

"You know, I just realized that you don't know anything about Gavin, do you?"

"No, I sure don't, but I bet you do."

And with that comment, Faith told the elder Gavin everything about his grandson that she knew. She smiled as she reminisced about her courtship with Gavin and how they were so in love. When she went through the timeline and arrived at the point of no return, she decided to not share why she and Gavin had broken up.

As if reading her thoughts, the elder Gavin asked her. "So why aren't you and Lil Gavin together anymore?"

"Like I said, it's complicated. Plus I'm here and he's there and it just wasn't meant to be."

"All right, I'll take that for now. But I have a feeling there's a lot more to that story. Plus I can see it in your eyes when you talk about Lil Gavin. You're not over him, are you?"

"Okay, if you're done eating, I think we can go now. I walked here so if you don't mind walking, we can go and get you checked into a hotel."

"Love is a touchy subject, huh. It's okay, young lady. I understand it's something you don't want to talk about. But you are going to have to deal with it sooner or later if you want to move forward."

Faith looked at him. Here was another person telling her that she needed to deal with her past. Why was everybody so bent on her dealing with the past? She would. But it had to be on her terms, not theirs.

"Yes, sir." She got up from the table and watched as Mr. Roberts gathered his assorted bags. She made a mental note to herself to pick him up some sort of luggage.

"Is that all your stuff?"

"Everything I own." He smiled.

"Let's stop off at Target and pick you up some necessities before we go to the hotel."

"Guess I don't have a choice since you said you weren't going to fight me on this." He chuckled.

"Nope, you don't." She grinned. They made eye contact again. He was indeed handsome. *So this is how Gavin will look when he gets older.* She smiled at the thought.

Chapter 8

Gavin paced around his apartment before dialing his mother's number. His mind was going a million miles a minute as he replayed the last call. This definitely was not how he imagined his first call from Faith or his first conversation with her. How could she have met his grandfather? Of all the people and all the places in the world, how did he just run up on his G-Pops like that? It had to be God he surmised. God wanted him and Faith back together. At least that's what he hoped.

He thumbed his favorites on his touch screen and the phone began to ring. It was a little before Noon in Atlanta on Saturday and he knew just where his mom Sheryl was.

"Hey, Gavin baby," she replied very loudly.

"Hi, Mom, you still at the salon huh?"

"Yep, my stylist was running late today, so I am still here. I'm sitting under the dryer now, so you're going to have to speak up."

Gavin rolled his eyes. Now was not the perfect time to be asking his mother questions about his father while she was under the hair dryer. Everybody at the salon would be all up in her business, but he had to. He needed to talk to his dad and find out why his grandfather was homeless in San Francisco.

"Mom, I have something to talk to you about and it's pretty serious, okay?"

"Okay, Gavin. But just speak up so I can hear you, baby. These old dryers in here are loud."

"Well, I got a call from Faith today and…"

"What…Faith called you? Now what's that about? You guys haven't talked since she left, right?"

"Yeah, Mom. That's right. But it's not about her calling me, it's about what she called me for."

"And what was that? Wait, a minute Gavin. Your sister is beeping in on my other line and Shelia is trying to check my rollers. I swear everything happens at once," she fumed.

She clicked over and came back quicker than Gavin expected. Normally his sister would have begged her to talk to her and call Gavin back, but I guess his mom was more interested in what he had to say.

"I'm back, Gavin. You know Gavanna was mad that I told her I would call her back because I was talking to you." She laughed. "You two will never stop your competing for my love. I love y'all just the same. I don't know why…"

Gavin interrupted her rant.

"Mom, listen to me. Faith called me because she met my grandfather in San Francisco."

The pause in his mother's voice spoke volumes. When it came to the Roberts family, she didn't have much to say, much less anything nice to say.

"So what, Gavin? She met him. What's the big deal? You already know how I feel about your father and his family…the little bit that he has," she said while mumbling the last part.

"I know, Mom, and I am not trying to bring up Daddy either because I know it's not something we discuss, ever. But when she called me and told me that she met him, it shocked me."

"Gavin look, you knew your father's father was in San Francisco, right?"

"Actually I didn't, Mom."

Sheryl waved him off. It wasn't something they talked about. Her son had been the man of the family as far as she was concerned. His father left them high and dry after Gavanna was born and was never reliable in any sense of the word. Sheryl didn't want to have anything to do with him, and she made sure Gavanna and Gavin held the same disdain for the man that she thought would have made a perfect father. She checked her judgment soon as he left them.

"Well, yeah, he lives in San Francisco. But don't you think for one minute that I want you running out there to meet him just because Faith met him. I realize you want Faith back, but this ain't it, honey. This is just one of those side tracks that get in the way of what you really trying to do. You don't have time to play catch up with your father's folks. If they wanted to know you, don't you think they would know you by now? You're twenty-two years grown, Gavin, and they haven't been a part of your life before now, so don't try to go there."

"Mom, I understand and until now, I wasn't interested in my dad's side of the family, but when Faith called and told me that she met him, I was initially shocked, but then she dropped another bomb on me. He's homeless."

There was that silence again, but this time Gavin knew the compassionate bones in his mother's body had been shaken alive, no matter how bad she hated his father for leaving her and the kids.

"What?" she exclaimed. "He's homeless?"

Gavin proceeded to tell his mother the entire conversation he had with Faith and how Faith was going to take him to get some food and put him up in a hotel.

"That was very nice of Faith. I see she still cares about you because not every woman would take an interest in her ex-boyfriend's long lost family member. I don't know what else to say, Gavin. What do you want to do because I know you already have some plan brewing in that little brain of yours and I bet part of it is to try to get Faith back."

"Very funny, Mom, but you're partially right. I just figured this is God's way of bringing us back together, you know."

"Did God tell you that or did you come up with that on your own and sign God's name to it?"

"Mom, seriously, please stop acting like I don't have a relationship with God. You know I have grown closer to God ever since I dated Faith. She was the one that helped me have a better relationship with Him."

"Yeah, I know the story, Gavin, and I am not making small of it, but I know you better than you know yourself, so don't be trying to force God's hand with Faith, okay. So what do you want to do?"

"Well first I want to talk to my father."

"Oh hell to the naw," she shouted. Every patron in the beauty salon turned toward her dryer. It was on now they all imagined. It was time for Saturday's salon drama.

"Mom, calm down. You know you still in the salon and everybody looking at you."

"I don't give a…Gavin, look, you ain't calling your daddy. I don't care if his father is homeless or not. I am not letting you reach out to that man who wants nothing to do with you. It's a recipe for disaster is what it is and I am not letting you fix that.

"Now as much as I feel for elder Gavin, I am not feeling you getting your heart broken over your father and his stupid ways. Don't you remember the last time we tried to call him?"

Gavin thought back to his high school graduation. He had been so excited to be graduating and going to Jackson State University to play in the school's famous Sonic Boom of the South Marching Band. He begged his mom to let him call his dad and invite him to the graduation and the after party she was throwing for him. After many no answers, she finally came around and said yes. But after the conversation Gavin had with his father, she wished she had left well enough alone.

"I remember how rude he was to me, Mom. But I was a little boy back then. I am grown man now and I can handle whatever he dishes out. If he comes at me with that same tired line of not wanting to have anything to do with us again, I'll be better prepared to respond. Plus he needs to know I'm a father now and that I don't plan to be anything like him when it comes to my daughter."

Sheryl listened to her son. He had definitely matured, but his last statement about him not being like his father worried her. Gavin and Chrissy hadn't been on the best of terms and when he told her last night that Chrissy was moving, she feared that the distance between them wouldn't be a good thing for the baby. But she prayed Gavin would still be a responsible father to his child no matter where she lived.

"Son, I understand. But please think about this before you call him. I know you want to help elder Gavin because that's a pitiful shame that he is homeless. I don't blame him for your father's actions because I do believe that if he and your father had ever had a decent relationship, elder Gavin would have wanted to be a part of you kid's lives. Just proceed with caution."

"I will, Mom. Now is his number still the same?"

"Gavin, I haven't talked to the man since I cursed him out after hurting you for your senior graduation. I don't even know if he is still here in Atlanta."

"Guess I will have to get on the internet and find out. I will talk to you later, Mom."

Sheryl took a breath. "Gavin, keep me posted."

She cared too and that was all the ammunition Gavin needed to proceed with his plans. He decided to call and let his sister know after he hung up from his mother. When his sister didn't answer, he figured the quickest dialing hands of the south had gotten to her already. His mom would fill her in on everything.

Gavin found two persons with the same name when he did a quick internet search. One listing had a Georgia address and the other listing was a California address. He keyed in the Georgia number and nervously waited through each ring.

"Yeah, who this?"

Gavin swallowed hard. *Here we go.*

"Hey, Dad, it's your son Gavin."

"Awe what's up, young buck. How you doing? It's been a long time, son."

Son. Gavin felt a smile creep onto his face. For most of his life, he secretly wished he could have had a relationship with his father. Maybe his father had changed.

"Nothing much, Dad. Well, actually, there is something."

"Now don't tell me after all these years you calling me for some money because I am going to be honest with you, I ain't got it."

"Nah, man, I am not calling you for money," Gavin said while rolling his eyes. "I'm calling because I just found out your father is homeless in San Francisco and I didn't know if you knew that."

"Homeless. Pops is homeless. Nah, man I didn't know that. Wait, how did you find out? You're in Mississippi."

Gavin was taken aback. "How do you know that?"

"Well didn't you attend Jackson State?"

"Uh, yeah, but I just graduated and…"

"And I know, son. You graduated with a degree in biology."

Gavin was confused. How did his dad know this?

"Look, son, your timing is perfect and I am glad you called. I have been meaning to give Sheryl a call to get your number. You must only have a cell phone because I have searched for your home number with no luck."

"Why were you trying to talk to me? You're not dying or anything, are you?"

"No, son, I'm not dying. At least I don't think I am. But I have changed my life and I am going into ministry and part of that process includes healing old wounds and mending broken hearts. I know I broke your mother's heart, and yours and Gavanna's, so I have wanted to contact you all. But since I hurt you the most, son, I wanted to contact you first before your sister."

Gavin could not believe what he was hearing. This was all just so much to consume at one time. He listened as his father talked about the new him and how he was now living in a small Georgia town about an hour from Atlanta.

"But, son, tell me more about Pops. I've been trying to reach him for the last year and have not been successful. Everyday I go through the death notices in San Francisco hoping he's not there, but it's like he dropped off the face of the earth or something. How did *you* find him?"

"Well I didn't. My girl…I mean ex-girlfriend did and she called me."

"You see, son, that's why I'm a saved man now. Only the God that we serve could make something like this happen. It was meant to be…for me and you to reconnect, and for me and my father to reconnect. The three Gavin's…it's time for us to finally mend our broken family." He cried.

The tears that had been forming in Gavin's eyes finally fell down his cheeks. He wept in silence. All of this had happened because of Faith.

After hanging up from his dad, he called his mother back, but she didn't answer. He needed to talk to somebody. He called Faith.

"Hey Gavin," she answered on the first ring. "Did you get in touch with your mom?"

Gavin began weeping again on the phone. This time he didn't cry in silence. He just let it out. Faith didn't know why he was crying so hard, but her emotions took over and she cried, too. She didn't know if she was crying because he was or because they weren't together.

"I talked to my dad, Faith," Gavin said through sniffles. "He's a changed man and he wants to be a part of my life. It's just all so surreal, Faith."

Faith had never heard Gavin cry so hard. She wished she was there to hold him and console him. This had to be tough on him. She remembered how it was when she found out about her real parents. Gavin knew who his parents were, but the emotional ties to reconnecting with family were overwhelming to say the least.

"It's okay, Gavin. Just talk to me. I'm here for you," she found herself saying.

Through more cries, Gavin tried to respond but couldn't. The built up emotions had overtaken him.

Faith just held the phone. He needed her and she was going to be there for him.

After about thirty minutes of tears and silence, Gavin stopped crying long enough to tell her about his father and their conversation.

"Well I have the number for Mr. Robert's hotel if you want him. I took him to Target to get some basics and gave him some money. He didn't want to take it, but I told him that I wasn't taking no for an answer."

"Yeah you have a way of making people do what you want them to do," he said, laughing. It was the first time he had laughed since talking to her. "Well my plan is to catch a flight and come to San Francisco. I am going to call my dad back and see if we can meet up there. What do you think about that?"

Faith hesitated before answering. Was she ready to be dealing with Gavin again?

"That's fine, Gavin," she nervously replied. "Just let me know your itinerary, and I will be there for you as much as I can." *Anything is possible with God.*

❦ ❦ ❦

Gavin began searching for a flight. He needed to get to San Francisco fast so that he could see Faith and rescue his grandfather.

He wanted nothing more than to repair all of his broken relationships - the one with his father and the one with Faith. Meeting his grandfather was just going to be the icing on the cake.

He felt the adrenaline running through his body. A checklist of things to do had begun forming in his head. *Pack my bags. Call Mom back. Call Dad back and suggest we meet there. What else?* Then it hit him…Chrissy and Grace Christian. He needed to call Chrissy. He wasn't sure when she was leaving, but he needed to work out something with her.

As he thought about how he would tell Chrissy that he needed some time to handle things in San Francisco, he thought about his daughter. He had been an OK father, but the more he thought about his father and the relationship of his father and his grandfather, he realized the trend. He didn't want to be his father. *I need to be a better parent to Grace Christian. I need to make sure I handle my business with her. She didn't ask to be here, just like I didn't ask to be here. I am not my father and I won't become my father. Maybe I can take Grace Christian with me to San Francisco. I bet Faith would love to see her and so would Chrishawn.*

Now he just had to convince Chrissy that was it. Chrissy, and her mother Charnese. But first, he needed to call his dad back.

≈ ≈ ≈

"Chrissy, it's Jameel. We need you to come up next week if possible. We have a meeting with the vendor from London on Wednesday. I know it is last minute, but we need you. Give me a call back and we can work out the details with your flight. Hopefully you can catch a flight out on Monday or Tuesday."

Monday or Tuesday? They are moving me way too fast. I told them I have a child to consider. Chrissy pressed seven to save the message.

She rubbed her temples. How was she going to pull this off? Being in New York next week was much earlier than she had planned, but they had been trying to get this meeting with the vendor in London for weeks. "Let me call Gavin. I know this is going to make his day," she said sarcastically.

Gavin answered on the first ring.

"Chrissy, hey. I was just about to call you. I gotta talk to you about something," Gavin rushed. He had just hung up from his father who decided to fly out of Atlanta. Gavin had offered to pay for the ticket, but his father said he could manage the airfare. Gavin was thrilled. This was going to be an exciting and very enlightening trip. He had so many questions for his father.

"Yeah, that's why I called because I need to talk to you, too. My trip to New York has been moved up."

"To when?"

"Next week," she nervously responded. She waited on the blow up from Gavin.

"Okay, that's no problem because the reason I wanted to talk to you is to see if it would be okay for me to take Grace to San Francisco."

Chrissy wrinkled her eyebrows in confusion. *San Francisco? Why would he be going to San Francisco?*

Before she could ask the question, Gavin explained.

"Oh I see. Well, let me run it by my mother and call Chrishawn. I don't have a problem with it. This actually works out for both of us. And I know Chrishawn is going to be thrilled to see Grace. So Faith is cool with all this, huh?"

"Yeah, she is," Gavin exclaimed. "I can't wait to see her, too. I mean, I know why I am going, but it's going to be great to reconnect with her."

"Gavin, you all haven't talked until today. I wouldn't be getting my hopes all up with Faith. I know Faith and she's probably just being compassionate about your grandfather situation. Don't mistake her compassion for you reconnecting your family to reconnecting with her."

Gavin didn't like what Chrissy was saying, but he didn't care. He was headed to San Francisco in a few days and he had hope that Faith would feel the same way he felt about seeing her. Excited!

"Let me know what your mom says, Chrissy. I am sure she won't mind, but I know she watches Grace all the time for us, so I didn't want her to be upset that I was taking her for a few days."

"Yeah okay, Gavin. I will. Hey, by the way, congratulations on reconnecting with your father. I know it means a lot to you. Many men who are raised by their moms long for days like this, you know."

"Chrissy, you have no idea what it means to me. And I have to say, too, that talking to my dad briefly today made me look at myself. You have been a great mother to our baby girl and my demanding you bring her to me wherever I land in school was out of line."

Chrissy could hear the sincerity in Gavin's voice.

"We are going to co-parent Grace the right way and I'm sorry we didn't work out as a couple, but she had nothing to do with that. She's the most important thing to me, and I know she's important to you, so we have to put our differences aside and raise her right. I don't want her to ever experience the hurt like I did. The hurt of not having a father be there."

"It's all good, Gavin. I'm moving forward to new things so everything happens for a reason. I will talk with you later."

Chrissy was glad that she hung up the phone when she did. The tears were about to come down her face. It was her that had wanted it to work out so bad with Gavin. But she knew deep down inside he never stopped loving Faith. He loved Grace and that meant a lot to her. Just like Gavin, she too grew up without her father. So he wasn't the only one. But she had to be strong. She was about to be in big-time New York City, a place where wimps got buried.

She could no longer allow the one night stand and her foiled relationship with Gavin define her anymore. She had to move on.

She could hear the pretend whistle in her head from her days as a majorette in the band at Jackson State: Tweeeeeet-Tweet, Tweet-tweet-tweet-tweet. *Forward March baby. Forward March.*

Chapter 9

*T*onight is the night. Tonight I am going to ask Faith to be my girl. Chrishawn and Faith had worshipped together at his church earlier that day, and he could see in her face that meeting Gavin's grandfather yesterday had her confused and thinking about Gavin. He needed to act quickly. They had been close friends since she moved to San Francisco, but now it was time to take things to a new level. The pastor had just preached about new levels of Godness today and He felt that God was telling him to take his relationship with Faith to the next level. If only he could get her to forget about Gavin.

"Faith, I need you to be ready at 7:30 okay?" Chrishawn requested.

"But Shawny, that's only an hour away. I just got back from ripping and running the malls to find this bridesmaid dress Aunt Jackie wants me to have. I am beat and I need to shower and…"

"Faith, sweetie. Just be ready okay."

She nodded. He couldn't see her, but she agreed in silence, then she spoke.

"Can I at least have until 8:00? Where are we going to eat any-way?"

"It's a surprise, woman. Now just be ready at 7:30. I know you know how to get ready fast. You do it every day for work." He laughed.

"Yeah, I know and I try not to do that on the weekends. But all right, all right. I don't want to mess up your little surprise. What's the occasion anyway?" she asked, knowing she wouldn't get an answer.

"Ha, ha, very funny. You already know the answer to that."

"Not answering is not an answer, but I will take that so I can get off this phone and try to get ready without rushing so much."

"Good. I will see you soon, sweetie."

Faith thought about Chrishawn and how sweet he was to her. Unlike Gavin, Chrishawn treated her like a lady. In Gavin's defense though, they were younger and less mature when they were dating. And Chrishawn *was* older. She liked him, but she wasn't quite ready to take things any further than friends. Especially not now. Gavin would be here in a few days and she needed to prepare herself for that.

"Tonight I want to make a toast. To the most beautiful girl in the world."

"Aw, that's sweet, Shawny. What are we toasting to?"

"I just said it…you Faith. For being the most beautiful woman I know, outside of my mother and sister." He laughed.

"Oh, I guess I thought you were going to say something else. By the way, this is a nice restaurant. How did you hear about this place?"

Faith looked around and noticed the waiters in their black jackets moving about from table to table. There was a large wine cellar in the middle of the restaurant that went all the way to the top of the ceiling. Their table, along with the other tables for two had red and yellow rose petals on top of the pressed white linen cloths. The ambience was subdued and the music in the background was barely audible, but just enough to set the tone for the place. Then Faith noticed that all the tables only had two chairs.

"Is this place strictly for couples or something because I just noticed there are only two chairs at each table in the whole entire restaurant." Faith continued looking around to make sure.

"Yes, that's right, Faith. There are only two per table at this establishment. Pastor Meeks, the marriage counselor at the church, told me about this place."

"Oh. OH!" she exclaimed when she had a moment to absorb what Chrishawn had just said. Her mind began racing and her heart was keeping up with it. *I know he is not about to propose. Oh my God, please not here, not tonight. I am not ready. We are not even a real couple or are we? Oh shoot, Lord, what I am about to do? What is he about to do? What is he about to say? Oh Jesus, help me.* Just as she zoomed her focus back on Chrishawn, he grabbed her hand. *Why did I have my hand available on the table? I should have had it in my lap. Oh God. I can't do this. Not now Lord. Not now. Not him.*

Faith felt herself getting ready to have a panic attack. She had never had one before, but this had to be what was happening to her. The room began to spin and she felt herself getting lightheaded. Before she lost it, she managed to remove her hand and dash away from the table. She left Chrishawn standing at the table. She had to get away and the ladies' restroom would have to do for now.

She pushed open the door and almost knocked down the restroom attendant. *This is a nice place,* she thought amidst her state of panic. As she made her way over to the closest sink, she searched frantically for the knob to turn on the cold water. She needed to dash her face with water. *That would help, right?* She was still breathing fast when she realized there were no faucets in the fancy marbleized bathroom. "Lord Have Mercy, how do you turn this water on?" she screamed to no one in particular.

"Just stick your hands under there and the water will come out," the calm voice said.

Faith looked through the mirror and noticed the older black woman standing behind her. It was the restroom attendant. Faith stuck her hands under the water and it flowed like a river. She let the warm water fill her hands then brought it to her face. *Ahhh.* There was the relief she was looking for.

"Are you all right, ma'am? You look like you are about to have a panic attack."

Guess that wasn't a panic attack since she just said I look like I am about to have a panic attack. Faith found her voice. "Yes, ma'am. I'm fine now. I just needed to catch my breath."

"Is everything okay at your table?"

"I don't know. I think my friend was about to propose, but I didn't give him a chance to do anything. I just bolted out of there," she said in still a rushed tone while holding her chest.

"I assume a proposal is not what you are looking for?"

"No, ma'am. It's not. He and I are just friends. And I am not ready for marriage. I'm not even sure I am ready to take our relationship to the next level. Wait. Maybe *that's* what he was going to do. Because how can we go from friends to engaged? That doesn't make sense. Oh my goodness, I feel like such a fool. I bet that's what he wanted to do," she said while leaning down on the bathroom counter with her head in her hands.

"Are you ready to be more than friends?" said the attendant as she moved in closer to Faith.

Faith kept talking to the attendant. She reminded her of her aunt. Warm. Considerate. Engaging. Caring. In those short moments, she felt safe talking to her.

"I don't know, ma'am," Faith respectful replied.

"Call me Erma."

"Well I don't know, Miss Erma. I just have so much going on in my head right now. I don't know if I can take on anything else."

"What is your name, dear?"

"Oh I'm sorry, Miss Erma. It's Faith. Faith Walker."

"What a powerful name, young lady. I know you are blessed and highly favored with a name like that. You definitely are very respectful because you keep calling me *Miss* Erma and that's rare these days."

Every time Faith told someone her name, they always had something to say about it. Usually it was church related. She normally didn't mind, but right now she wasn't up for entertaining how unique her name was.

"Yes, ma'am," she said with raised eyebrows hoping Erma would catch the clue that she wasn't interested in talking about her name.

Erma may have been older, but she was very mindful and noticed Faith's demeanor. "Well anyway young lady, God won't put more on us than we can bear."

Faith shifted to her left foot. Her high heels were starting to hurt. She knew just what Miss Erma said to be true. She had survived some stuff in her life and she knew that God was always with her.

"Thanks, Miss Erma. You're speaking my language now for sure. Guess I just needed a quick reminder that my life is not my life. It's what God wants it to be. I don't have time to tell you the details or my life story because I am sure Chrishawn is out there waiting for me, wondering what's wrong."

Just then the door cracked opened and Faith heard her name.

"It's okay, Chrishawn. I am on my way out. Give me a few minutes."

"Okay, because girl I was just about to come in there and get you."

"Oh no you weren't," Miss Erma responded with a grin. "No men are allowed in the ladies' restroom, son."

Faith snickered as Miss Erma winked backed at her.

"Thank you, Miss Erma. God put you here to get me back in check."

"Awe, sweetie pie, you're welcome. I meet some interesting ladies in this restroom you know. Some coming in happy. Some come in sad. But either way, when they leave, I try to make them feel glad…glad that they encountered someone nice. So that's why I keeps a smile on my face. You never know who needs one."

Faith smiled back at Miss Erma.

"Anytime you're eating here, be sure to come in and say hi."

"I sure will, Miss Erma. You take care," Faith said while giving the woman a tight squeeze. "Now let me get on back out here. I'm starving!"

"You're in for a sweet treat, my dear. The food here is excellent."

Faith made her way around the nicely adorned small tables. She spotted Chrishawn standing near their table with a big grin plastered across his face.

"And what are you smiling about?" she asked.

"The fact that you are the most beautiful woman in this place. And believe me; I've had enough time to see the entire place, waiting on you to come out of that restroom. Why did you bolt away so fast anyway?"

Chrishawn gestured for Faith to sit and she obliged.

"Look, Shawny. I didn't know what you were about to do. Fear gripped my chest like a vice grip and the only thing I could do was run. I thought you were about to propose to me and I felt like I wasn't ready for that."

Chrishawn raised his eyebrows. "Propose? Are you serious, Faith? You thought I was about to propose to you?"

"Yeah. And why are you acting like that's so out of the question?" She frowned.

Chrishawn smiled a devilish grin. He had her just where he wanted her when she asked that question.

"Exactly, Faith. It's not out of the question. But I am glad you realize how much I care about you. I am not ready for us to go down the marriage road, but I am ready for us to commit to each other as a couple. We've been friends and I want more. Faith, you're such a beautiful person inside and out. You're saved, successful in your career, and you've got a big heart. I love those qualities about you. I know we've been through a lot, mainly you, but I am ready to take our friendship to the next level. To the level of courtship. Will you be my girlfriend?"

And with that, Chrishawn pulled out a black square velvet box that housed a heart ring in between the two soft, white, satin pillows inside.

"Now this isn't an engagement ring, as you can see." He laughed. "But it's a heart ring because I want your heart… and I want you to have my heart."

Faith felt the lone tear stream down her face. Now here was a man that truly cared for her and listened to her, but all she could think about at that very moment was her heart and how it still longed for Gavin. *Lord help me to let Gavin go and accept Chrishawn.*

"Well Faith. Will you? Will you be my girlfriend?"

Waiting on the Lord to guide her, Faith eyes darted around the restaurant and noticed Miss Erma coming out of the restroom. She gave her thumbs-up and a smile. That was it. That had to be it, right? God was confirming it.

"Yes, Chrishawn. Yes, I will be your girlfriend."

Chrishawn rose halfway from his seat and leaned over the table to seal the deal with a kiss. Faith closed her eyes and accepted his lips as they pressed against hers. She squeezed her eyes tight when images of Gavin appeared. *God, please help me. Help me to move forward.*

Faith sat at her desk admiring the gold heart ring. It was indeed a beautiful ring, but she was still torn about accepting it. She had gotten the confirmation from God when Miss Erma gave her thumbs up or had she? Feeling confused, she decided she would immerse herself into her work.

"Girl, I know you didn't get proposed to and didn't tell nobody!"

Anastasia must have seen Faith through the glass admiring her ring. She really didn't feel like dealing with Ana today so Faith gave her one of those serious work looks.

"Is there something you need, Ana? I'm really busy with this new campaign, and I need to really stay focused so that I can beat my deadlines."

"Oh so now we really acting funny, huh. You done got your big deal and your big proposal because you ain't always had that heart ring sistah girl. And now you want to act all shady with ya sistah. That's cool, Faith. I gotcha. Don't worry 'bout me, girlfriend. I'll let you be so you can handle your business."

Ana stood there waiting for Faith to respond. *Now didn't she say she was going to let me be?*

Not one to be offensive, Faith made eye contact with Ana and gave an innocent eye roll.

"If you must know nosey, this is not an engagement ring. It's a…"

Faith found herself at a lost for words when she tried to describe the ring to Ana. What was it? A friendship ring? She gave up trying to identify the ring

"Anyway, it's a heart ring that my boyfriend Chrishawn gave me. We've decided to take our friendship to the next phase."

Ana swarmed around Faith's desk and gave her a half hug. "Oh my goodness, Faith girl. That is so sweet," she sang. "Girl, I knew that you guys were going to really hit it off eventually. He is such a sweet person. He and I talked at your party and he is very spiritual and stuff like you. I know you two will make a great couple. Especially since you're both from the same hometown, right? And I think he told me that his sister is your best friend back home?"

Faith really didn't feel like having this conversation.

"Well, what all did he tell you at the party?" Faith asked.

"Oh nothing much, that you two were friends from back home and you both moved here around the same time and that you and his sister were best friends from high school and college. I think that was about it."

Faith breathed a sigh of relief. Why was she worried anyway. Chrishawn would never tell her business to a stranger. She didn't want anyone knowing about her past relationships. Especially not an office gossip like Ana.

"Oh yeah, he also told me that he's liked you for a long time, but you were dating some other guy and he never had the chance until now to get to know you better. So who was this other guy you dated? You never told me about any exes you had. I always thought you had always been married to your work the way you act around here."

Ana leaned over onto Faith's desk with her elbows. "So tell me, Faith. Who is this ex of yours and why did y'all break up?"

Faith had had enough of Ana. "Didn't I just tell you that I am busy? And my past is really none of your business, Ana."

"Whoa, whoa, whoa, Miss Mississippi. I thought we were girls. I mean we are the only two AAs here you know. So I just figured we would stick together, you know what I'm saying. I know we ain't on the same level career wise, but we both still black and women in an industry that ain't full of us."

Faith felt the olive branch that Ana was extending. Ana was right. There weren't many women, let alone African American women in the industry and they were they only two at Elite. As much as Faith wished that Ana wasn't so unprofessional, she felt obligated to her as a sister friend.

"All I am saying Ana is that I am not trying to rehash my past. That's all. I get where you are coming from with us being AA sisters and all, and that's cool, but I like to keep work at work and home at home, if you know what I mean."

"Ok, I gotcha, girl. So you want to catch up after work and chit chat. I am up for happy hour anytime you are."

That's not really what Faith meant, but she was just ready for Ana to leave her office, so she agreed.

"Okay Ana, I don't drink, but we can have dinner sometime in the near future."

"All right cool. Plus I want to run some ideas by you that I had for the Shay Praise account. I think you might like some of what I gots to say."

Would she please stop adding an "s" to her words?

"Sounds good. We'll chat more later."

Ana left Faith's office and Faith turned her chair to face the window. She was relieved that Ana was gone, but she still had that heart ring to deal with. She told Chrishawn he had her heart, but she knew deep down that she needed her heart to be mended before it could be given away again.

Mend my heart, Lord so that I can move forward. Help me Lord because Gavin will be here tomorrow.

Chapter 10

"From the flight crew of flight 777, we would like to thank you for flying Southwest Airlines, where LUV is in the air. Sing it with me now. Love is in the air…"

The flight attendants kept singing as Gavin looked over at Grace sitting like a big girl in her booster seat. She was peering out of the airplane's small window and smiling back at her daddy. He was glad that she had done so well on the long flight. She'd slept most of the way.

The plane landed and pulled into the jet way. Immediately when the doors opened, Gavin grabbed Grace and her bag and headed down the jet way toward the terminal. Faith was supposed to be meeting him in baggage claim. Deep down he was more than thrilled about seeing Faith. He pulled out his cell phone and turned it back on. He had three missed calls from Chrissy. "I knew that girl wouldn't give me a chance to call her before she ringed my phone. Grace, let's call Mommy before she puts an APB out on us." He laughed.

"Gavin, are y'all okay? Where is Grace? How did she do on the flight? What took you so long to call me? You know I am over here worried sick about my baby."

"Would you calm down. Grace is fine. She's with her daddy you know, and I won't let anything happen to my girl. We just landed and I just turned my phone back on right before I called you. We are only running five minutes behind our scheduled arrival time. Geez girl."

"Now Gavin you already know this was Grace first time flying and her first time going out of the state of Mississippi. So don't be acting all brand new on me. I was worried about my pookie pooh."

"There you go with that ghetto name calling. She is not a pookie pooh. Please stop calling her that."

Gavin and Grace headed to baggage claim.   "Look, I need to find a family restroom so I can get my girl situated. I will call you back once we find Faith, okay."

Chrissy obliged and hung up the phone. Gavin and Grace freshened up near baggage claim and just as he was coming out of the restroom, his cell phone rang. It was his father.

"Hey, son, where are you? I'm in baggage claim and I've been here for the last hour. I was able to catch an earlier flight."

"Okay, I am in baggage claim, too, just coming out the restroom. Tell me where you are."

"I'm over here near the smoothie shop next to the big California souvenir place. You can't miss it. They have a huge sign that says California Souvenirs."

Gavin made his way toward the neon sign. His father was right; you couldn't miss that place if you tried.

"Dad?"

Gavin's father turned around just in time to see Gavin and Grace walking up to him. He knew it was his son. They looked almost identical; except for a few gray hairs in his father's beard, they could have been twins.

"Son, is that you?"

Just as Gavin was about to answer, Grace reached out her arms and yelled Daddy. It was confirmed. Gavin Jr. and Gavin number three were finally together.

"Wow, son, you and I could be twins."

"Yeah, Dad, I didn't know we looked this much alike. I mean, I knew I looked good and was handsome and all, but I didn't know I got it all from you."

"And, son, I got it all from my dad."

As the three of them continued to fellowship, Gavin's phone rang. This time it was Faith.

"Hey, Gavin, it's Faith."

"I know your voice, girl. I'm here at the airport. Where are you?"

"Looks like we are coming your way right now."

Gavin looked around in search of Faith all the while wondering who *we* was. As soon as he spotted her beauty among the crowd of people, his eyes moved down her body and saw her hand enveloped with someone else. It was Chrishawn.

Gavin felt himself biting his lower lip. *How could she bring him? I knew we would see him since I have Grace and all, but what was this hand holding they had going on? Faith didn't mention that she was with Chrishawn when we talked. I would think she would have mentioned that.*

"Is that my niece Grace I see?" Chrishawn exclaimed as he released Faith's hand. Gavin was relieved to see him do that.

Gavin Sr. handed Grace over to Chrishawn. "Excuse my manners, sir. I'm Chrishawn, Grace's uncle. You must be Mr. Roberts?"

"That would be me. Well at least I am one of the three." He gave a hearty laugh.

Faith stood there among the men and noticed the similarities of Gavin and his dad. She remembered the elder Gavin and thought about how estranged they each were to each other, but how they all looked so much alike.

Gavin motioned for a hug from Faith and she obliged. "It's so good to see you, girl. You're still looking as beautiful, if not more beautiful as ever. I see California has been really good to you."

"Yes it has," Faith answered shyly. She felt so awkward and she knew she would. Last night she had prayed to God to help her get through this very moment. She had to admit though, Gavin was looking really good. In between her wandering eyes, she noticed his fresh haircut. Not wanting to stare, she looked at everything else but Gavin.

"So, how you been? How's work? You took off today I suppose?"

"Yeah, I did. I figured it would be too much to try to pick you all up and then go meet elder Gavin and try to work. How was your flight? How did Grace do on the plane?"

Faith watched as Chrishawn played with Grace. She still hadn't met Gavin's eyes and figured it would be safer that way.

"Oh, she did great. Of course she slept most of the way, but she was a real trooper."

"Cool," Faith replied. "Well, I have lunch plans set up for us at a neat little spot and we have to pick up elder Gavin at the hotel. You and your dad are staying at the same place, so you can drop your stuff off there. Chrishawn wants to take Grace back to the church with him while you all meet, if that's okay with you. He said he cleared it with Chrissy for him to spend some time with her while you get reacquainted with your dad and granddad."

Why was she acting like this was a business transaction? Then Gavin noticed the ring on Faith's hand. *What is that?* He needed to get her alone. As much as he wanted to bond with his father, that much of him also wanted to reconnect with Faith. For him, this trip was two-fold; reestablish his relationship with his family and reestablish his relationship with Faith. He just hoped it wasn't too late.

While Gavin retrieved his and Grace's luggage, he saw Chrishawn and Faith talking. He wondered what they could be talking about. Faith was smiling and laughing and so was Chrishawn. Grace was playing with her stuffed bunny on the floor in front of them. This behavior between them made Gavin uncomfortable. He knew Chrishawn and Faith were cool, but this was too cool for him.

He kept watching them and watching for his bags.

"Son, is this your bag?" Gavin's father asked.

Gavin directed his attention back to the conveyor belt. His bags had been around twice and his father saw that his attention had not been on retrieving his bags, but on Faith.

"Oh yeah, Dad, that's me." Gavin reached for the bags and hoisted them off the belt and pulled the lever to roll them over to where all the giggling was.

"So are we ready to go?" he gladly interrupted.

"Oh yeah, okay. You got all your stuff?" Faith asked nervously.

"Yep, right here. And here is Grace's bag, Chrishawn."

"All right, I appreciate, that man. I can't wait for all the ladies at the church to see you, pretty girl," Chrishawn told Grace as they started walking toward the car.

Gavin began following them until he noticed Faith still standing there.

"I'm sorry, Gavin. I drove my car here, too. Chrishawn just met me up here to pick up Grace. I'm parked over here. You and your dad are riding with me. Come on this way," she said as she found the strength to move in the direction of the parking garage.

Just as they began walking away from Grace and Chrishawn, Gavin remembered that he needed to give Grace a kiss.

"Yo, Chrishawn, hold up a minute, dawg. I need to give my baby girl a kiss goodbye."

Gavin went over and kissed Grace and told her he would see her later and to be a good girl for Uncle Chrishawn. Just as he released his daughter's embrace, he caught them. Faith had just given Chrishawn a kiss on the lips. *What in the heck?*

"I will call you later, baby," Chrishawn nearly yelled. He knew what he was doing and so did Faith. She was totally uncomfortable and ready for this moment of awkwardness to pass.

"So you and Chrishawn are an item now, huh?" Gavin asked. "Is that why you haven't been able to return my calls?"

Faith really didn't want to discuss her newly formed relationship with Gavin, especially not in front of his father. She decided to bring Gavin Sr. into the conversation, totally ignoring Gavin's quietly posed question.

"So Mr. Roberts, are you excited that you and Gavin have reconnected? I know this trip is going to be so awesome with the three of you all coming together...all the Gavin's." She smiled.

"Oh yes. I just can't believe how quickly all this came about. But the God I serve can do anything. Shucks, I am still in awe of God's goodness. Me and my boy here are finally going to be the father and son we were meant to be. And I am finally going to be a righteous son to my father. Ain't God something?"

"He's everything," Faith replied.

Gavin watched from behind as Faith and his father walked together and kept chatting about the goodness of God. He hoped God would be good to him and give him his Faith back.

Faith pulled her black C-Class Mercedes into the Hilton Suites parking lot. Before they could even park, she saw elder Gavin coming out of the glass double sliding doors. He had been waiting for them.

When he saw Gavin the third and Gavin Jr., the tears started pouring from elder Gavin's eyes. Faith felt herself began to cry. It was the best reunion she had ever seen. Here were three generations hugged up in a hotel parking lot crying like newborn babies.

Faith watched the men and began to feel out of place. She decided it would be better to have their lunch delivered and for her to go back to work. She needed to get away from Gavin. She knew what he wanted to know. She told the men of her plans and Gavin was too caught up in the moment to notice her quick exit. Seeing his grandfather made him suddenly realize what was happening in his life. He was finally getting to the root of his family tree and his manhood.

Faith drove back to her loft. Work would have gotten her mind off of Gavin, but she didn't feel like being bothered with her co-workers.

She knew Ana would be all in her face and she wasn't up for that, not after all that she had just endured with the Roberts men reunion and her reunion with Gavin.

She walked into her bedroom and noticed the journal. *I haven't written anything in it in a while. Maybe I can work through these emotions with a little writing.*

Dear Journal,

Today was kind of weird. I was with Chrishawn, but when I saw Gavin, my heart nearly stopped. I know he's not the one for me. At least I think I know. I am not sure if I am honest. I just don't know why God would bring him back to me if he wasn't for me. But then I know God is not the author of confusion. Lord, I'm writing Dear Journal, but this is really a letter to you. I need you to help me understand what I am supposed to be doing. Gavin is here. Chrishawn is here and has given me this heart ring and I have accepted his request to be more than friends even though deep down I am not sure I am ready to be in another relationship. I don't know God, but I know you do. Can you tell me what to do?

Faith stopped her pen and waited for God to answer. She knew he spoke to her conscious, so she waited. While she was waiting, her phone rang. At first, she thought to ignore it, then she decided to see who it was. Maybe God was going to answer her through the person on the other end of this phone.

She peered down to look at the Caller ID. It was Gavin.

"Hello."

"Hey Faith, it's me Gavin. I just wanted to call and tell you thank you so much for all that you have done. After the cry fest you witnessed, my dad and my granddad and I came up to the room and have been talking non-stop. I told them I needed to step away a minute to call and thank you. They both wanted to thank you as well. Faith, I love you for just being who you are."

Faith held the phone. The cry fest was now at her doorstep. Her voice was inaudible. She couldn't say anything back to Gavin. Her heart was saying I love you, but her mouth said nothing. She just held the phone while Gavin continued thanking her and telling her how much he loved her still. *Was it possible to love two people?*

❧ ❧ ❧

Gavin was on the west coast and Chrissy had just touched down on the east coast. Chrissy was missing Grace already. She didn't want to keep calling Gavin, but she wanted to check on her baby girl. She knew Grace would be staying with Chrishawn the first night, so she figured when she got settled into the hotel, she could give Chrishawn a call.

Chrissy noticed the sign being held by a young Puerto Rican man. The sign read: Chrissy Jackson. She smiled at the cute driver. It was the black town car her company had sent to pick her up from the airport. She rolled her large suitcase toward the man. When they made eye contact, he knew she had to be Chrissy.

"Ms. Jackson I presume?" he said with a dimpled smile.

Oh my goodness he is too fine.

"Yes, that's me." Chrissy handed him her luggage and he opened the back door for her to climb in. The black leather seats were cool to the touch and the car smelled of fresh vanilla bean, one of Chrissy's favorite scents.

As the driver closed the trunk and headed to the driver's side of the car, Chrissy watched him take off his jacket. He leaned in and threw it on the passenger seat and peered back at Chrissy.

"Ms. Jackson, I hope you don't mind if I drive with my coat off."

Chrissy was speechless as the man smiled at her while waiting for her to respond.

She found her voice when he raised his eyebrows as if to suggest that she hurry up and answer.

"Oh, uh, yeah, that's no problem. Whatever makes you comfortable, Mr."

"You can call me Armando, Ms. Jackson."

"And you can call me Chrissy, Armando." *Armando.* Chrissy enunciated his name silently as he turned around to watch the traffic for a clearance to pull out from La Guardia's passenger pickup area.

"We're still going to Sugar Hill Harlem Inn, right?

Chrissy pulled the emailed itinerary out of her purse. She read the hotel information.

"Yes, that's correct, Armando." She liked saying his name. It was different and she had never met anyone in Mississippi named Armando.

He laughed and Chrissy frowned.

"May I ask why you are laughing?" she asked in her proper voice.

"I'm sorry, Ms. Jackson, I mean Chrissy. It's just that you sound so different from the women here in New York. May I ask where you are from?" he asked with a heavy Puerto Rican accent.

Now how is he going to say I sound different? He's the one that has an accent.

"I'm from Mississippi. You ever heard of the south?"

"Oh yes, I've been to Texas a few times before, but I pretty much stay here in New York most of my time and my life. I moved here when I was little boy."

Chrissy just loved his accent even though his English was slightly broken. As the two continued to talk, Chrissy got a picture mail message on her phone. It was Chrishawn. He had taken a picture of Grace. She smiled to herself. That was exactly what she needed; confirmation that her baby girl was doing just fine away from her and her mother.

As Armando maneuvered his way through the streets of New York, Chrissy wondered how Faith and Gavin were doing. She knew Gavin wanted to get back with Faith, but her brother had already told her about his plans. She smiled a devilish grin. Gavin had no idea what he was up against, trying to convince Faith he was the better man. If she knew anything about her brother, he was a fighter and this time, he was going to fight to keep Faith. He had waited much too long to get her to let Gavin come to town to take her away.

Chrissy hoped that since Faith and her brother were closer now, it would help her and Faith get back to being best friends. True, she had broken the biggest best friend rule ever by sleeping with Gavin and having his baby, but their friendship was much bigger than her mistake. She had let go of the past, but she knew Faith really hadn't. Her prayers were that God would bring them back together as best friends. She missed talking to her. But now that her brother and Faith were an item, it was only a matter of time.

"We're here," Armando announced, breaking Chrissy out of deep thought. Chrissy peered out the window at the historic hotel. Her manager had wanted her to experience true Harlem and this was definitely it.

Armando removed Chrissy's bags and carried them inside for her. She was definitely enjoying this preferential treatment.

"Unless you need me tonight, I'll be back to pick you up to take you to work in the morning," he announced.

For a split second, Chrissy let Satan contaminate her mind with a lustful thought. *Stop it, Satan!*

"Okay, that will be fine. I'm not very hungry so I should be straight."

"Well here is my card if you change your mind about tonight. I'm just a phone call a way if you need me, Chrissy."

"Thanks, Armando. You've been very kind." Chrissy removed a ten spot from her purse and handed it to Armando.

"Oh no, Ms. Chrissy. I won't take tip from you, ma'am. It was my pleasure to drive you. Plus your company has already taken care of everything, including tips." He winked.

And with that, Armando hopped down the steps and got back into his black town car and drove away. Chrissy turned to the hostess who had her welcome package ready. She would be staying in the Lena Horne room, one of the most elaborately designed rooms at the historic bed and breakfast.

After taking a relaxing bath, Chrissy called Chrishawn to say goodnight to her angel Grace. She had a big day tomorrow at work, so she kept her conversation short. She wanted to ask Chrishawn about Faith, but that conversation would have to take place another time.

After hanging up from Chrishawn, she knelt down on the beautiful hardwoods to say her prayers. New York was about to be her new home. Tomorrow would be her first day working at corporate headquarters, and even though she had made great impressions while telecommuting from Jackson, this was an opportunity of a lifetime and she did not want to blow it. Chrissy climbed into the bed. She left the light on so the beauty of the old Harlem Renaissance room could be seen until her eyes fell shut.

Chapter 11

"Finally, the weekend is here!" Giselle said as she rolled toward her husband in the bed. "Honey, wake up. You need to get that grill going. We got a lot of people coming over here today and I want that meat to be falling off the bone. So get up!"

"Come on, baby. I got time. It's going to be good, I promise," he said while cuddling up with Giselle even more. "Give me a few more minutes. You had me working so hard last night that I just need a few more minutes of sleep, baby."

Remi's reference to last night made Giselle smile. She hoped that last night's lovemaking would produce a baby.

"All right, but only because you were so wonderful to me last night. I am so glad that we waited until we got married to be intimate, Remi. It makes everything so new and so right."

Snoring ensued and Giselle stopped her ranting. Remi had fallen asleep just that fast.

Giselle wanted to get a jumpstart on her part of the BBQ meal, so she got up and showered. She needed to chop the vegetables and prepare the side dishes. Plus she had to wash all the new outdoor dishes she had just purchased at Garden Ridge. She couldn't wait for the festivities to start. This would be their first time hosting a party at their new home and everybody they knew were coming by.

∽ ∽ ∽

"Well Mr. Smith and Ms. Walker, I'm glad you two could show up for pre-marital counseling. As a pastor, I highly recommend that all couples get premarital counseling before they walk down the aisle.

And I make it a requirement for all couples that I marry. So let's get started you two. Tell me, how did you two meet?"

Jackie peered at Darnell before deciding to take the question herself and answer it. She thought he looked so handsome in his khaki pants and white button down shirt. Jackie wanted him to dress nicer than his usual blue work Dickies, and Darnell was happy to oblige.

"Well Pastor, I know we are only scheduled for an hour session, so I will give you the quick version of our story. We met when we were young. We dated for a while and I got pregnant and Darnell was not ready to be a father, nor was I ready to be a mother. I was on my way to school to get my master's degree in teaching and a baby was not part of the plan. Plus Darnell was on the road to becoming a total deadbeat and I didn't want a child with him."

Pastor Wright looked at Jackie in a peculiar way. He wasn't expecting this kind of story because it sounded like it was to have an unhappy ending the way Jackie was telling it.

"Okay, continue," he admonished cautiously.

"So anyway, I made the decision to have an abortion and…"

"Whoa, Ms. Walker. I, um, didn't know…"

"Oh no Pastor, it's not like that. You see, here is the blessing. I was going to have an abortion and I didn't tell Darnell, but I called my brother to ask for the money. That very day, he and my sister-in-law found out that she couldn't have kids. When I told them what I was planning to do, they offered to raise Faith. That's our daughter's name, Faith.

"Anyway, Faith grew up in a loving home with my brother and she grew up thinking I was her aunt. I doted on her like a true mother would, but I never told her this family secret. Now this story could get long, but again, I know we don't have a lot of time here. So anyway, Darnell and I hadn't spoken in over 20 years, that was until God brought us back together when Faith found out about me being her real mother. You see, Darnell was dating Faith's best friend's mother."

Pastor Wright held up his hands. He had held countless premarital counseling sessions, but this was by far the most confusing one he had ever encountered. "Wait a minute. So your daughter was raised by your brother and sister-in-law, am I right so far?"

"Yes, that's right, Pastor."

"And you dated your daughter's best friend's mother?"

"That's right, Pastor," Darnell said, "but I didn't know I even had a daughter."

"Whew wee, this is a doozy here. Glad I drunk my green tea because y'all are making my brain work overtime today." He laughed. "Ok, continue on, Jackie."

"Well after a series of circumstances, Darnell and I were reunited, our daughter was told the truth and Darnell and I have fallen in love all over again and are ready to be married." Jackie took a deep breath as if to say, that's the story. She rested back in the chair.

"I must say, you two do have a story, one that is most interesting. I can say that I've never heard anything like that before. As we move through this counseling session, the first thing I want us to do is take an oath that we will be honest about everything. I know you two were together a long time ago, but there is much time between when you first dated and now. I want you to take me down the journey of your lives apart and your lives together as a couple now. Let's leave no stone unturned. Is that okay with you both?"

"Yes," Jackie immediately answered.

Darnell began squirming in his seat. He popped his neck to the right and to the left, then starting biting his bottom lip. Jackie looked at him suspiciously.

"Darnell, are you okay with what I have just asked of you?" Pastor Wright asked again.

Darnell looked at Jackie and took her by the hand. "Yeah, I'm cool with that." He nervously smiled.

The lump Jackie felt forming in her throat went away when Darnell answered. Jackie settled back into her seat.

Pastor Wright was a certified counselor and when he noticed Darnell's foot tapping uncontrollably, he made a note of it. *He's hiding something*, Pastor Wright wrote on his notepad.

"Let's see how far we can get today. Pull out your bibles and turn with me to Ecclesiastes, chapter four, verse 12."

When Darnell removed his hand from Jackie's, she noticed the amount of sweat that had formed in his hand. The lump in her throat came back.

    ⋘   ⋘   ⋘

"Remi, where is my iPod? I know you had it last," Giselle shouted upstairs.

"It's in the truck, baby. I'll get it when I go outside unless you have to have it right now."

"I need it right now. I need some upbeat music up in here." Giselle made her way out to Remi's hummer. *He needs to get his own iPod and stop stealing mine.*

As she made her way back into the house, she heard Remi on the phone. "Yeah that's no problem, the more the merrier," she heard him say." *Who was he talking to?* They had tons of food, but she didn't want everybody in Houston at her house. She already didn't know half of Remi's friends who were coming anyway.

"Hey baby, that was ReRe. She said her sister wants to come, too. I told her that was cool, but what's strange is I grew up with her and I didn't even know the girl had a sister. She said that her grandmother raised her sister in Louisiana because her sister was like the black sheep of the family and her parents couldn't discipline her. Isn't that something, baby?"

"Well it's not unheard of in Mississippi for a grandmother to raise a wild child. But it's funny that y'all were friends and she never ever mentioned it."

"Nope, not a single word. Guess if her parents told her not to say anything, she had to hold that secret."

"Guess so. Anyway, can you get your own iPod and stop taking mine?" She playfully smacked him on the butt.

"Even if I get my own, it won't have the same music as yours. And I like that cool gospel music you got on there. Man for real though, that music sounds like R&B and Hip Hop."

"I don't care if it sounds like drip drop, stop taking my stuff, Mr. Aguilar." She rolled her neck.

Remi laughed as he walked off. He loved him some Giselle, and she knew it, too. He turned back and winked at her. She couldn't help but blush. She loved him so much. If only that love could extend into a baby, that would make her life complete. She rubbed her stomach. Maybe their baby was already in there. She smiled at the thought.

∽ ∽ ∽

"Son, you really outdid yourself with this BBQ," Remi's mother exclaimed. "And this sauce is so good."

"Now I can't take credit for the sauce. That's the wifey's doing there, Momma. Giselle says that Texas BBQ is not better than Mississippi BBQ. I told her that's because they douse everything in sauce. They don't really care about the rub and the seasoning because it's all sauced up. It can be the worst meat in the world, but if you got good sauce, she thinks it's good BBQ." He laughed.

"Well with your seasoning skills and my sauce skills, we make a great BBQ. We should probably start selling it. These people in Texas have no idea about good BBQ sauce."

More people continued to pour into the party, but Giselle still hadn't seen this ReRe person yet. She still wanted to see the mystery woman who had said those things to her on the phone.

Giselle reached for her strawberry drink and a piece of BBQ Rib fell off her plate onto her khaki pants. "Ugh, would you look at this?"

"See, baby, all that dang gone sauce." Remi laughed. "If you had just had seasoned meat, you wouldn't have to change your clothes."

"Whatever, Remi. I'll be back y'all," she announced to the table. As she made her way back into the house, she noticed a car pulling up. She'd have to meet and greet after she changed clothes.

Remi's dad saw the car pull up, too, and noticed the two women getting out. It was ReRe and Reyna.

"Oh my goodness," he mouthed silently through clenched teeth. He jumped up and Remi's mother noticed his uneasiness as he scooted around the table. "Uh honey, I am going inside to refresh my drink. I'll be right back."

Rohan quickly rushed toward the house, his wife watching his every move. He hoped he could cut the women off before they arrived to the back of the house. He noticed Remi heading over to the grill to retrieve more food. If only Rohan could speak to Reyna before she came back there.

Just as Rohan went through the back door, he heard the doorbell ring. Since the back gate wasn't open, everyone that came over that day had to come through the house. "I'll get the door Giselle," Rohan screamed.

"Okay, Dad, thanks because I am still changing," Giselle answered from the master suite.

Rohan opened the door and nearly snatched Reyna's arm off when he led her inside. ReRe was left standing at the door looking puzzled. While both women were identical, Rohan had been dealing with Reyna for so long, he knew her from her sister.

"What the hell are you doing here," he mouthed angrily after dragging her into the home office and shutting the French doors behind him. "What happened to our agreement? Didn't I tell you that I didn't want you anywhere near my son, huh? Didn't I tell you that as long as I was taking care of everything, you didn't need to have any business to do with my son?"

Reyna snatched her arm away and straightened her spaghetti strapped tee. She rolled her eyes. "Humph, you've messed up now, old man. Nobody touches me like that and gets away with it."

"Reyna, girl you're going to make me really hurt you. I thought we had an iron-clad agreement. You stay away from Remi and I take care of you and Recio. Why are you here, Reyna? Tell me, what tricks do you have up your sleeve by showing up here to my son's home with his wife, family, and friends around. What do you hope to accomplish today, you conniving…"

Before Rohan could finish, ReRe opened the doors to the office. "Uh, what is going on here?"

"Nothing, ReRe, I'll be out in a minute. I just had to talk to Mr. Aguilar about some real estate stuff he was working on for me, that's all. I will be out in a minute. Go make sure there is some BBQ left."

ReRe knew her sister was lying. After all, this was her twin sister and she knew something wasn't right. She was going to leave well enough alone for now, but she was definitely going to find out later. Her sister had always been a trouble maker and she could tell by the angry look on Mr. Aguilar's face that Reyna had done something. She just didn't know what it was, *this time.*

As soon as the door closed and ReRe was out of sight, Reyna took control of the conversation. "Look here. I am over here with my sister. Don't worry, Mr. Aguilar. I am not going to say anything to ruin you or your little knuckleheaded son. My lips are still sealed as we agreed. But the next time you get the nerve to touch me again like that, you can be assured that your secret will become major news."

While the two continued talking, Rohan's wife, Charlotta stood nearby eavesdropping. *What in the world is going on,* she wondered.

Giselle made her way back outside and noticed Remi talking and laughing with someone. Her back was to Giselle, so she couldn't see who it was. But Remi was smiling like a Cheshire cat, so she made her way over to the grill. Just as she got close enough to see, Remi saw her.

"Hey baby, come on over here and meet my old high school buddy, ReRe."

ReRe turned around. Giselle's face looked like she had just seen a ghost. Her eyes were widened and her mouth was hanging open. Remi's smile turned into a look of utter confusion.

"Giselle, why are you looking at ReRe like that? Honey, you act like you've seen a ghost or something."

Giselle moved her mouth to respond, but before her words were uttered, Reyna announced herself to the crowd. "Hey good peoples, how is everybody doing?"

ReRe rolled her eyes at her flashy sister who always had to be the center of attention.

Everyone looked at them, but not the way Giselle kept looking back and forth at the two women. Remi couldn't believe his eyes. Other than their hairstyles, they looked exactly alike.

"Remi, this is my sister Reyna," ReRe announced. "Remember I told you earlier that I would be bringing her," she said with a bit of regret in her tone.

Remi snapped out of his obvious trance and greeted Reyna. "Hi, Reyna, it's nice to meet you. Wow, you and ReRe look just alike."

Reyna turned to Giselle. "And how are you, Giselle? Didn't see you at the office yesterday. Were you there?"

When Rohan heard this, he almost choked on his drink. Reyna was working with Giselle? He felt his head starting to hurt. The tension in his temples was working overtime and he wanted to drag Reyna out of there before things got out of his control. He already felt like her simple presence there was at the border of being uncontrollable.

"So Reyna, you work with my wife?" Remi asked.

"Oh yeah we sure do. I just started not too long ago, but I love my new position." She grinned mischievously.

Remi sensed Giselle's uneasiness and put his arm around her waist. "So Reyna how long have you been in Houston?"

"Well after growing up with my grandmother in Louisiana most of my childhood, I decided to move back to my original home. Of course my family didn't quite welcome the black sheep back home, but I've been here for several years now."

"So did you attend college somewhere in Louisiana?" Remi probed. For some reason he wanted to know more about Reyna.

"Yeah I have a degree if that's what you are asking, Remi. Otherwise I wouldn't hold such a high position at Heights Publishing. I went to school mostly at night since I have a son and…"

Before Reyna could finish outlining her resume, Rohan interrupted her by clearing his throat.

"Uh son, I need to run a few errands for work. Did you still need some more ice for the coolers? I can pick it up while I am out."

"Oh yeah, Dad. Thanks."

"Uh Reyna, I think you all are blocking me in," Rohan said while pointing toward the front of the house and bucking his eyes as if to say, meet me out front. "You mind following me to the front so that I can get out?"

Rohan was proud of his quick thinking to remove Reyna from the party. Once he got her to the front of the house, he would demand that she leave and stay away from his son as he instructed her four years ago when she came to him wanting to get Remi's contact information.

❧   ❧   ❧

It had been a crazy day at the office when Reyna showed up. Rohan had been in and out of meetings all day and wasn't expecting an unknown visitor. She walked in with dark black shades dressed to the nines in her black slacks and white button down, looking more like a young executive than a conniving blackmailer, seeking to make his life a living hell.

Rohan's assistant had been out that day and when Reyna showed up carrying a young baby in a car seat carrier, Rohan's first thought when he glanced up and saw her was maybe she was lost and looking for some help in the right direction. Their office building had a lot of different companies, so he figured she was on the wrong floor.

"I'm looking for a Mr. Aguilar," she spoke confidently outside his office.

He couldn't see her face that good as he peered around his desk. Initially confused and bewildered by her request for him, Rohan spoke up. "Yes, that would be me, how can I help you?"

Quickly shaking his confused state of mind, Rohan surmised that she may have wanted to become a client. She was young, and he shouldn't have assumed that her age made her less likely to be one of his high dollar clients.

She walked in and sat the baby carrier on his desk and stated, "This is your grandson, Recio, and I need your son Remi's information so that I can tell him about his son."

Rohan retracted his neck and looked at her in disbelief. "ReRe, is that you?" he asked her, still confused.

Having grown up down the street from the Smith family, Rohan recognized who he thought was Remi's childhood friend ReRe Smith. "ReRe, I haven't seen you in a while. What is this you are talking about and why are you acting like you don't know me."

Reyna responded roughly. "That's because I don't know you, man. All I know is that your son and I slept together during spring break and produced this baby, and I need his information so that he can take care of his child."

Now shocked by her demeanor and total disrespect, Rohan held up his hand.

"Now hold on, ReRe…"

"I am not ReRe," she screamed at him. The newborn baby was sleeping and didn't move, not even after she screamed.

"Well you look like her." Rohan started thinking about split personalities. He had not seen ReRe in a long time and maybe her life had taken some bad turns and she was losing it or something.

"I am her twin sister, you idiot!"

"There's no need to be disrespectful, young lady. You come in here demanding my son's information saying this is his baby and you expect me to just hand it over and go on with my day? Then on top of that, you look like the little girl that grew up down the street from me and expect me to know that ReRe has an evil, I mean a twin sister," he quickly corrected himself.

"Look, all I know is this is your son's baby and we need to be taken care of."

Rohan didn't like this situation at all. He wasn't sure if this was his son's child or not, but he made a hasty decision that he would handle this problem for his son. Knowing his son was the heir apparent to his real estate throne, he decided to be the financier that Reyna was looking for. Not one time did she say she wanted his son to be a loving father. She only wanted money.

That's when Rohan made a rush decision and decided to offer her a nice package of hush money. "Look ReRe, I mean Reyna. My son is in college and he is not prepared to be a father. I would be the one taking care of this baby, so why even involve him. You don't seem to want a father for this baby; you just want to be, in your words, *taken care of.*

"So consider me the person to handle my son's financial business. But there is one catch. If I am to financially provide for this child that you say is his, then you won't have any contact with my son. I will provide you with a monthly check to handle the needs as long as you never speak to my son again ever."

Reyna bit her bottom lip contemplating the offer Rohan had just presented to her. She didn't really know Remi, and all she really wanted was for her and her baby to be taken care of. *Why not?* she surmised. *If I can get what I want from this old man, then I could be set for life.*

"That's fine. Just make sure I get my money on time every month and your son never has to even know this child exists."

Rohan shook her hand and instantly felt like he had just made a deal with the devil. Reyna smiled and took the baby carrier and walked out.

"What Reyna wants, Reyna gets," she said as she got on the elevator. Rohan watched the doors close behind her.

"Don't worry, Recio, we're set for life, little man," she said as the elevator descended.

⤜ ⤜ ⤜

That was four years ago, and Satan had come back to renege on the deal. Even after Rohan had fallen for every one of Reyna's tricks, including getting her a house in one of the most expensive areas of town, Reyna still wasn't satisfied. He should have never made that deal with her. He wasn't even sure if Recio was his grandson. If Remi ever found out that he hid his child from him, the wonderful father-son relationship they have would be ruined. And not only Remi, but his wife Charlotta would probably kill him. They never kept secrets from each other.

Rohan nearly lost his mind when they got to the front of the house. "Look here, girl, you are going to leave this party and never return.

You are going to quit your job at Heights Publishing because I don't want you anywhere near my daughter-in-law. I'm not playing with you, Reyna. If you ever want another dime, then you will do as I say and leave my son alone!"

Charlotta watched this exchange and knew something was going on. She had her ways of finding out information and her husband wasn't going to be the first person she asked. She went back to the party. She needed to have a little talk with her old neighbor ReRe.

"ReRe, so how have you been, girl? You looking good," she said.

ReRe was preoccupied with trying to figure out what was going on with her evil twin sister and didn't seem at all interested in Charlotta's attempts to make small talk. "Oh I've been well, Mrs. Aguilar. This is a nice home that Remi has here."

"Yes, it is. I helped him and Giselle decorate it. They've been preparing to add to the flock and I can't wait until Giselle gets pregnant. I think I have the grandmother bug. I see that ring on your finger, are you married?"

"Oh, no, ma'am. It is an engagement ring though. My boyfriend or should I say fiancé couldn't make it, so I brought my sister."

Jackpot, Charlotta thought. She brought up her sister. Let the interrogation begin.

"Yes, that is so weird that we didn't even know you had a sister. All that time we lived near you guys and we had no idea. So tell me more about her."

ReRe was somewhat reluctant to talk about her sister. She wasn't proud that her family had hid her from everybody, but Mrs. Aguilar had always been a sweet person to her, so she felt she could talk to her. Maybe Mrs. Aguilar knew why Reyna and Mr. Aguilar were talking earlier.

"Well, my sister and I are like total opposites. You know me. I am shy and more reserved and she's loud and boisterous. She always has to be the center of attention. She was a problem child, so my parents sent her to live with my grandma. Of course my grandma could barely contain her, but she always took her to church and prayed for her. I don't think it helped, but Reyna is just Reyna. I love her as my sister and I want us to be close, but we're just so polar opposite."

"Yes, I understand, dear. You two look alike, but are nothing alike."

"Exactly." She laughed. "But one thing good that has come from Reyna is her son Recio. I love that little boy to death. He's what keeps me connected to her. Otherwise, she and I would only have looks in common."

"Oh, she has a son, huh. Is she married?" Charlotta probed.

"No, ma'am. She had Recio out of wedlock. We don't really know who his father is, if you know what I mean. Reyna's kind of out there. But in any case, Recio is a blessing. He's very respectful and seems to take after me because even at four years old, his demeanor is very reserved, thank God."

Charlotta continued talking to ReRe and soaked in every detail about Reyna. Giselle noticed her mother-in-law entrenched in deep conversation with ReRe, and her father-in-law in serious conversation with Reyna out front. *What was going on here?*

Remi was too busy talking to his boys from high school to even notice any of this exchange, but Giselle had a bird's eye view. She felt in her spirit that something just wasn't right about these twins. ReRe seemed to be nice, but that Reyna was just as mean as she was when Giselle met her at work.

Reyna returned to the party and announced that she had to leave to pick up her son. ReRe wasn't ready to go, but since she and Reyna were together, she said her goodbyes and walked out with Reyna. When they got in the car, she asked Reyna the obvious question.

"So what's going on Reyna? Why were you all up in Mr. Aguilar's face, huh?"

"ReRe, you are so dang gone nosey. But if you must know, we were talking real estate okay. I was asking him about refinancing my mortgage."

"I thought you told me when you got that house that you don't have to pay a mortgage?"

"Dang girl you remember everything, don't you?" Reyna laughed. "I don't have to pay it, but my friend who pays it told me to check on getting it refinanced and I wanted to ask Mr. Aguilar since he's in real estate. I called him before about it, so that's why he was talking to me like he knew me. My friend who got me the house knows him anyway."

ReRe knew her sister was lying. She could feel it in her twin bones. *Lord, why are we so different?*

ReRe accepted her sister's lie. "All things done in the dark will come to light, Reyna," she said.

"Girl, would you just shut the heck up?" She yelled. "You and your twin senses get on my nerves sometime. You think you know me, but you don't. We're sisters, but we don't have to be friends, ReRe, okay?

"I thought this would work, but you work my nerves a little too much. I won't keep you from spending time with Recio, but as far as we are concerned, let's stop this charade of trying to be best sister friends and just live our lives separately like Mommy and Daddy made us when we were kids."

ReRe felt her eyes water up. She loved her sister, but only God could help their relationship at this point.

Chapter 12

Reyna slammed the back door that leads into the kitchen as she entered her home. "Oowee, I hate him!" she screamed. She started throwing anything she could put her hands on. A pen flew across the room. Then the roll of paper towels followed it. Then she dragged everything from her kitchen island to the floor. When the plate crashed to the floor, Recio started crying.

"Oh, Mommy's sorry, baby. I'm just a little upset with your grand-daddy right now. Go on in your room and play, okay, baby? Mommy is going to bring you a Popsicle in a few minutes."

Recio quickly dried his tears when he heard the word Popsicle. It was the cure to all his four-year-old problems. He started toward his room and came running back. "It's going to be okay, Mommy. I love you, so don't be mad, okay?"

Reyna looked at Recio with love spilling over in her eyes in the form of tears. He was definitely her little man. She gave him a kiss and he happily trotted off to his room.

She had let Rohan have his way by making her leave the party before she was ready to leave. But she had another plan up her sleeve; Rohan and his son would get theirs soon enough. She laughed to herself as she thought about her plans to torture Giselle at work. She'd heard around the water cooler that Giselle wanted to be pregnant more than anything in the world. *Just wait until she finds out that her little hubby already has a baby.*

She grabbed a purple Popsicle for Recio out of the bottom freezer drawer. She had one of those fancy stainless steel refrigerators with the two double doors on the top and the freezer on the bottom. It had been another purchase by Mr. Aguilar. She smiled as she ran her finger across the edge of the $2000 appliance. "I'm not evil, I just want what's mine," she said aloud. She stepped over the mess she made during her tirade and took Recio his cool treat. She had some planning to do. *Everyday is going to be hell to pay.*

≪ ≪ ≪

Darnell was glad to be out of the pastor's presence. It was almost like the pastor could tell he was hiding something. Probably because he was. He paced around his apartment. Jackie would be calling him soon for their nightly chat, and he needed to shake this guilty feeling before Jackie caught on.

If I could just finalize the divorce before next month's wedding, everything will be all right. The Divorce. Those two words had been plaguing Darnell every since Maria called him two days ago.

"Darnell, this is Maria," she said with a heavy Hispanic accent. "How are you, señor?"

"I'm doing real good, Maria. How about you? It's been a long time since I heard from you. What have you been up to?"

"Well, señor, I am calling because I have a problemo."

"Okay," Darnell replied hesitantly. He was scared to even ask, but he did. "What's going on?"

"Well, I think the authorities are coming to do their periodic check up, and I need you to come stay with me again."

"Oh come on, Maria. They haven't checked on us in nearly three years. Why do you think they are coming to do a house visit now?"

"Because my friend told me that she got checked recently. Please, señor, I just need you just this one and no more. I promise. I give you more money, please, señor."

Darnell hated that he had let Maria convince him to help her out. He was going through some hard times and the $5000 payment was music to his ears when Maria approached him about marrying her to get fast citizenship.

For six years, Darnell periodically played step-in husband to Maria, who kept her apartment looking as if Darnell stayed there. He even had to get his place in his sister's name to thwart off any additional checks from the United States Citizenship and Immigration Services office. So much time had passed since Darnell last saw or talked to Maria, he had forgotten about her and their fake marriage. He hadn't thought about his marriage to her until she called him. Now she wanted him to play husband again. He had to get a divorce. Sooner than later.

"Look, Maria. I really had forgotten all about this fake marriage, but we have to stop this. I need a divorce. I proposed to my girlfriend and we are getting married in October, which is next month. We have got to get a divorce, Maria."

"But, señor, I just got my citizenship and if we get a divorce now, we could be in much trouble. I could get deported and you could go to jail for fraud."

"Now, I ain't going to nobody's jail. You got me in this mess and you're going to help me get out. Who do we need to talk to, Maria, because I have got to get a divorce before Jackie and I go down and apply for a marriage license. I know they're going to check to see if I am married and the answer needs to be no. Dang! I bet they are going to show that I have been married. Oh my God! How I am going to tell Jackie about this? I need to tell her before she finds out."

"You don't need to say anything to anybody right now. Look, señor, let me talk to some people and see what we can do. I just know that if we make it seem like we just got married for me to get my citizenship, we are going to be in big big trouble."

That two-day old conversation with Maria had been replaying in Darnell's mind like a broken record. He needed some help from the Lord to get out of this mess. Quick.

Before the conversation could play again in his head, his cell phone rang. He knew it was Jackie from the Lionel Richie ring tone dedicated to her. "You're once, twice, three times a lady," the phone crooned.

"Hey, baby, what's going on?"

"Oh nothing, just sitting here amidst all this wedding stuff. Who would have thought planning your own wedding would near 'bout kill you." She laughed.

"Yeah."

"Baby, what's wrong? You don't sound yourself. Plus you were acting weird at Pastor's office. Are you going to tell me or am I going to have to drag it outta ya?"

"It's nothing, Jackie," he said. "Nothing I can't handle," he whispered to himself.

"Darnell, look, we can't be going into this marriage not communicating, baby. If there is one thing that I have learned from other people's jacked up marriages and TV talk shows, and that is we must communicate. Plus, that's how we got in trouble the first time, not communicating with one another. Whatever it is, baby, I am here for you. I know you know that, right?"

"Yeah."

"Okay, so spill it, man. What is ailing you?"

He took a deep breath. *Maybe I should just go ahead and tell her now instead of after I get it worked out.* Then a deep voice spoke to his conscience: "Man, you better not tell her. She's going to break up with you for sure and then you won't have anybody. And you know if you get caught with this marriage scam you're going straight to jail. Just keep this little secret from her.

"What she don't know won't hurt her. This happened before her, it's in your past, man. You just need to focus on how you're going to swindle some more money from Maria. You know this wedding is costing you a lot of money. Take Maria for some more change and then marry Jackie. It'll be all good."

Darnell listened to the voice and decided to lie.

"Baby, I just think I am really nervous about being a husband and I got cold feet. I didn't want to say anything to you because I figured you wouldn't want to hear it."

Jackie paused before she spoke. There was a brief silence over the line.

"Baby, you there?"

"I'm here, Darnell. So are you saying you want to cancel the wedding?"

Darnell shot up off his black leather couch. "Oh no, baby, I am not saying that at all. I'm just saying that I'm scared, that's all."

"Are you sure that's all it is, Darnell? You don't have any dark secrets that you are hiding, do you? I mean we're going to get our blood tests done in a few weeks and I don't want any surprises."

"Baby, no." He laughed. "I don't have any kind of disease or anything. I'm just nervous. Aren't you nervous, Jackie?"

"I guess so. I've been so consumed with the *planning* of our wedding, I really hadn't taken the time to just reflect on the fact that we will actually be married. Guess it's good we are going to premarital counseling so that we can get all this out before we take the plunge."

"Yeah, guess so," Darnell responded.

There was a long pause and then Darnell said the three magic words that always made Jackie feel better. "I love you," he whispered loud enough for her to hear but silent enough to sound sincere.

"And I love you back, Darnell. We're going to be fine. As long as we keep God first, stay honest with each other about everything and communicate about everything, we will be just fine, baby."

"Yes, baby, you're so right."

"You know what, Darnell. Let's say a prayer now. If we say we are going to keep God first, we have to actually make Him first."

"Okay baby. Are you going to pray?"

"Yes. Father God, in the name of Jesus, we ask that you will keep us. Lord we are about to go to the next level in this relationship and get married. Father, we know that as long as we keep you first, everything will be all right. We ask that you give us strength, patience, guidance and protection as we move forward with our plans to become one.

"Lord, you said marriage is honorable and we want to be everything you want us to be in this marriage, especially honorable to one another. Help us to always tell the truth to each other and keep our lines of communication open. We rebuke the enemy and every evil strategy he tries to throw our way to keep us from serving and honoring you in our marriage. Lord, you know our hearts. You know our fears. Keep us Father in your keeping care and we will forever give you the praise, the honor, and the glory. Amen.

"Amen," Darnell responded.

"Whew, I feel better already, don't you, baby?" Jackie said happily.

"Jackie....I...I....I'm married already to someone else."

Chapter 13

Chrissy had been in New York since last Tuesday and had seemed to already have learned the ropes of the big city life. Armando had been teaching her how things worked and she had loved every minute of it. Her next priority was to find a place to live. Her managers had given her some recommendations and Armando had offered his suggestions as well. She had her list and was going to check out a few spots today.

Since it was Labor Day, she didn't have to work, so she called Armando to pick her up. Her job was still letting her use Armando's car service, but he probably would have picked her up for free, even if he wasn't getting paid.

Chrissy had learned so much about Armando in the last few days and was impressed that he owned the car service and wasn't just the driver. He didn't have a huge clientele, but he was doing pretty well from her vantage point.

"Armando, do you know where this place is?" Chrissy said while pointing to an address on her list.

Armando leaned in close and she could smell his cologne. It was Sean Jean's Unforgiveable but it should have been called *Unforgettable* because it smelled so good on him.

"Oh yeah, chica, I got you. Let's ride out."

Chrissy jumped in the front seat of the town car this time. She wasn't feeling the Driving Miss Daisy, ride in the back, routine today.

As they made their way through Harlem, her phone rang. It was Chrishawn.

"And how's my baby girl doing?" Chrissy grinned.

"Oh she's fine. I can't believe Gavin has let her stay with me the entire time. Guess he needed a parental break, too." Chrishawn laughed.

"Well, I don't know about that. Momma is always keeping her for us anyway. What's my little angel doing?"

"She's taking a nap right now. But when she gets up, Faith and I are going to take her to the San Francisco Zoo."

"Oh that sounds like fun. Glad to hear that Gavin ain't crampin' your style being in town."

"Nah, I got a handle on brother man. I'm more concerned about Faith though. I think once we get out from under Gavin today, she'll be more in tuned to me like she was before he arrived."

"If she hasn't completely let him go, it's going to show now that he's in town. I know my girl. We haven't been talking lately, but if I know anybody, I know me some Faith. I'm just glad to know that you are there for her. She deserves to be treated with respect, just like me. And speaking of being treated, I gotta let you go, big brother. Armando is taking me around town to look for a place." She grinned.

"Um hmm, every time I've talked to you since you arrived in New York, his name has come up. Is there something you want to tell me, sis?"

"Not yet." She laughed. "But we shall see. Holla at you later."

"Bye, crazy girl."

Chrissy looked over at Armando who was really focused on maneuvering through the traffic, and then he caught her staring and winked at her. She bit her lip to keep from smiling so hard. *Thank you, Lord. I don't know what you got in store for me in New York, but I am thanking you in advance.*

᭡   ᭡   ᭡

Faith knew Gavin really wanted her to hang out with him and his family today. Everybody was leaving for home. She also knew Chrishawn was planning a trip to the zoo for her and baby Grace, but a part of her wanted to be with Gavin. *It's like I don't have true closure, God.*

After stepping out of the shower, Faith poured lotion on her body, sprayed her neck and wrists with Dolce and Gabbana's Light Blue perfume. It was still her favorite fragrance. She had tried other perfumes after moving to San Francisco, but nothing else matched the light and clean smell of D&G. It reminded her of home.

She put on her dark blue jean capris and her red v-neck cotton t-shirt and slid her feet into her red crocs. *I at least need to call Gavin back and tell him that I can't hang with them today.*

She dialed Gavin's number. When she heard a phone ringing on the other side of her door, she frowned. Faith looked through the peep hole. Gavin was at her door. Her heart began to race. She looked around her apartment and then she heard the knock.

"Uh, who is it?" She knew exactly who it was, but she didn't know why he had come by unannounced.

"Faith, it's me Gavin."

Faith turned the double deadbolt locks and slowly opened the door. She peeked out like she was sneaking a look. Gavin leaned in toward the opening and met her peeking eyes. He could already smell her sweetness and it brought a smile across his entire face.

"Hey girl, why are you peeking like you sneaking trying to catch somebody creeping or something?"

"Well, I didn't know I was going to have a visitor."

"Yeah, I thought I would just surprise you. Can I come in or are we going to continue this conversation in your hallway?"

Faith bit her inner jaw in contemplation. "Um, I think I can let you come in for a minute."

"Thanks. I'll be sure to leave in the next 55, 54, 53," he kept counting the seconds as Faith gave him a crazy look.

"So what's up, Gavin? What are you doing here?"

"I wanted to come by and hang with you for a minute. I talked to Chrissy and she told me you already had plans with Chrishawn for today. Guess it would have been nice if you could have told me that instead of her."

"I was planning to call you as soon as I finished getting ready, which I just finished."

"Um hmm…I can smell…I mean I can tell." He laughed. "So I guess you were going to tell me, no, huh," he said and flirted with her with his big doe eyes.

Oh God, here we go, she thought. "Gavin you already know there is no us. I mean, you do know that, right?"

"Do you really believe that though, Faith?" He took a seat on her sofa. She kept standing, nervously.

"Yes, I do, baby," Faith said before she even realized that she called Gavin baby. It felt so natural to her lips. It rolled off her tongue like it used to.

Gavin's eyebrows rose when he heard the word. He smiled and she knew she had made a huge mistake letting him come in. She plopped down beside him on the sofa in defeat. He reached for her hand. As much as she didn't want to, she relented and fell into his chest. *Lord, did you bring him back to me?*

The two just held each other for what seemed like an eternity. Both had their eyes closed and were crying silent tears.

Chrissy was moving to New York with his baby girl. Chrishawn was moving in on his favorite girl. Gavin didn't want the moment to end. He squeezed Faith tighter. Then out of nowhere, he spoke.

"Faith, will you marry me?"

❧   ❧   ❧

Chrishawn buckled Grace into her car seat and rushed around to the driver's side. He was glad he and Faith could have some time of their own together finally. As soon as he took their relationship to the next level, Gavin showed up. He knew Gavin wasn't any good for Faith, but he knew Faith hadn't let him go 100 percent yet.

He started up the engine and pulled out of his apartment's garage. He had tried to call her twice, but she hadn't picked up the phone. She knew what time to be ready, so he and Grace made there way to her place.

"How you doing back there, niecy?" Chrishawn asked Grace. He peered through the rearview mirror at her and she happily played with her toys. She didn't have a care in the world.

"Sweetie, you just don't know. You are an angel from God. Your life is going to be so blessed. Your mommy loves you so much, and she is making some moves so that you two can have a great life."

Grace smiled at him and continued playing with her toys. Just as he was about to take the Bay Bridge exit, his phone rang.

"Hello?"

"Hey Coach CJ, this is Jerrell from the Youth Center. Coach Thompson said we needed to call you because he's not able to take us to our game this afternoon. Can you take us?'

"Uh, well, I…"

"Oh please, Coach CJ. This is our first baseball game of the new season and if we don't have a church van to take us, some of the players might not make it. Then we would have to forfeit if we don't have enough players there. Plus I think we have to have our team sponsor there to play anyway."

Chrishawn pulled over before making the exit to the bridge that would have taken him across the Bay to San Francisco where Faith lived. How was he going to handle this? He was the Youth Director and he didn't want to let the boys down.

"Jerrell, what time do you guys have to be at the church to ride to the field?"

"In an hour."

"Okay, I'll be there," Chrishawn stated.

"Thanks Coach CJ, you're the best, man."

Chrishawn quickly tried to call Faith again. Hopefully she would pick up this time.

"Hello," she answered with a sad tone that Chrishawn picked up right away.

"Hey, baby, what's the matter?"

Sniffles.

"Nothing Chrishawn. Sorry I missed your call, but I…"

"No need to apologize baby. Look, I have Grace with me and we were headed to get you, but I just got a call from the boys at the church and Coach Thompson can't be their sponsor today so I told them I would. Can you meet me somewhere? I need you to watch Grace until I can get in touch with Gavin and let him know that I can't keep Grace today."

"No need to call Gavin. He's right here."

Chrishawn rolled his eyes and sulked down in the driver seat of his blue Chevy Malibu.

"I don't even want to ask why he is over there, Faith. Can y'all just meet me to pick up Grace? We can talk later," he said with a stern, but semi-polite voice.

"Okay," she answered unapologetically.

"I think it would be easier if y'all came over here to Oakland to meet me. How about you meet me at the church? I don't have to drive the boys for an hour, so Grace and I will be there."

"All right. We'll be there soon."

Faith hung up the phone and Chrishawn stopped short of throwing his phone in disgust. *Why was that dude over there,* he thought. "Grace,

your daddy thinks he's slick, but God is not the author of confusion.
I know Faith and I are going to be together because God already told
me so. And I know this little hurdle that your daddy is creating is just
temporary." Grace smiled back at him. She looked so much like Gavin
when she did, Chrishawn rolled his eyes. He squeezed the steering
wheel tightly in frustration. He made a quick call to his little sister.

"Guess what?" he said into the phone before Chrissy could even
say hello.

"What?"

"Your boy is really trying to get Faith back. He's over there right
now and they are about to come and meet me because we can't take
Grace to the zoo because the boys at the church need me."

"Chrishawn, slow down. Now what now?"

"Basically, I can't spend any time with Faith today because the
youth at the church need me. And Gavin is over to Faith's house right
now. I don't know how long he's been over there, but I tried to call her
twice when Grace and I were on our way and she didn't pick up."

"Calm down. Just give it some time. Gavin will be gone tomorrow."

"Yeah, he'll be physically gone, but I don't think he will be mentally
gone from Faith's mind."

"Look, you already said God told you to marry Faith, so why are
you letting this upset you? If God told you she's your wife, then move
past this moment."

"I know. I know. It just burns me up that he's here."

"Well if he wasn't there, you wouldn't have Grace there." She
laughed

Chrishawn peered back at Grace. This time when she smiled at
him, he didn't see Gavin at all. He just saw his angelic niece.

"You right, sis. I guess I just let him get the best of me for a
minute."

"It's understandable, but just stay focused on Faith."

"No, I gotta stay focused on God. For a minute there, I felt my old ways coming on. You know, my old thuggish ways."

"Now don't go trying to be the Chrishawn of the past. God has brought you a long way and he didn't bring you this far to leave you now. I know he didn't bring *me* this far to leave me. It's going to be all right, Chrishawn. For real. For real."

Chrishawn laughed. "You always think saying something twice makes it that much more believable, don't you?"

"Yep. Yep," she laughingly replied.

"All right, sis. Thanks for the pep talk. I'll call you later."

"Okay, bye."

"Later."

Chrishawn pulled back out onto the road and headed toward the church.

৶   ৶   ৶

"So Faith, are you going to answer me or do I need to get on one knee?"

Faith had started collecting her things to leave. "Look, Gavin, that question was so out of line and inappropriate. Me and you, right now, this right here…all of this is just inappropriate. I let myself go for a minute and the devil came right on in and made himself at home."

"Faith, I love you though. And I know you still love me."

Faith retrieved her keys from the hanging rack and nearly pulled the rack off the wall. "Gavin, look. You are right. I do still have love for you, but this is all just confusing, and I know God don't make stuff confusing. I made the choice to move forward with my life and your being here is just a test to see if I am going to trust God.

"Me just happening to meet your grandfather. You coming here. All of that was just part of the test. I can't let your being here these few days make me go backwards. I am marching forward, Gavin, and I pray that you will, too. Come on, we gotta go and get Grace."

Gavin didn't move from Faith's couch. He put his head in his hands. "What do I have to do, Faith? What do I have to do to get you back?"

Faith stood at the couch waiting for him to get up. She took a deep breath and put her hands on her hips. "Gavin, we need to go and get your daughter."

"We can leave once you tell me what I can do to get you back," he stubbornly replied.

"Gavin, we have to drive to Oakland and if the bridge is packed, we won't make it in time and Chrishawn has responsibilities at the church. Please let's not do this now, okay."

"If not now, then when, Faith?"

"Gavin, seriously, I am about to leave you here and go and get *your* daughter since you can't seem to be a responsible father right now."

That hit a nerve. Gavin got up without a saying a word and headed to Faith's door.

"Let's go then," he said while ushering her with his hand out of her own place.

The bridge wasn't packed so they made it to Oakland before Chrishawn left. Both men were mad at Faith. Neither one said a word to her when they first arrived. She focused her attention on Grace.

Chrishawn broke the silence. "The game should be over in about two or three hours, then I'm taking the boys for ice cream. I will call you once I am done."

"Okay, that's fine."

Chrishawn leaned in and kissed Faith on the lips. She responded positively and Chrishawn felt his anger began to subside. It was Gavin's turn to focus on Grace.

Gavin buckled Grace in and he and Faith were off. "So where are we going?" she asked Gavin.

"I guess you can take me and Grace to the hotel. My dad and granddad can spend some time with her now that the plans for today have changed."

"All righty then," she said in a cheerful tone.

"Why are you so happy, Faith? We have unfinished business to discuss and it doesn't look like we're going to get it finished today."

"Gavin, honestly, we don't. I'm done and I'm with Chrishawn," she responded even more cheerfully than before.

"So that's it, then?"

"That's it, Gavin. I'm moving on."

She continued to drive toward the Bay Bridge. She tapped her fingers on the steering wheel to the tune of the music coming from her iPod. She had it connected to her car radio. Mary Mary's *It's the God in Me* was playing. The way she felt so free, she knew it had to be the God in her at that moment. She sang along to the tune while Gavin just watched her profile. As the song ended, gospel artist Israel Houghton's *Moving Forward* began to spill from the speakers. And there it was. Her confirmation from God.

Chapter 14

Reyna got to work early at Houston Heights Publishing. She needed to put her plan into motion as soon as possible. She grabbed her coffee cup and headed to the kitchenette. Since she was the first person there, she had to make the brew herself. She opened every drawer before she found the filters. *This place is so unorganized.*

She filled her red and white mug with the savory black substance. Before leaving, she poured so much sugar and cream into her coffee, the color was khaki brown when she finished. She pressed her small light brown lips on the cup and took a mini sip. *Perfect.*

As she made her way back to her office, she stopped by Giselle's desk to take a look around. She noticed the picture of Remi on her desk. She nosed around her calendar and notebook and noticed some of the things Giselle had written down.

"My goodness, this girl wants a baby bad, doesn't she." Reyna laughed. Trying not to move anything out of its proper place, Reyna looked for anything she could use against Giselle, but she couldn't find anything. *Oh well, I will continue with the plan I have.* Reyna walked to her desk, sat down and took a sip of the sweet, hot substance. She opened up a new memo on her email program and began to type:

Hi Susan, just wanted to follow up with you regarding my ideas to boost employee morale. I was thinking we could either have bring your child to work day or go bigger and have a company picnic where we invite our families to attend. I can definitely be on point to spearhead either suggestion. I would love to discuss these further with you. I know you wanted to do something soon, so maybe we can do both. The "bring your child to work" day is probably the easiest to implement. All we would need to do is send an email blast to all employees. Look forward to hearing back from you. Reyna Reynolds.

"There, that should get things going up in here." Reyna smiled. "We'll see how little miss sunshine feels when she can't bring a child to work on bring a child to work day."

Reyna clicked send and relaxed in her black high back chair. *This is going to be so fun watching her squirm.*

Giselle was late coming in to work. Her dentist appointment ran a little longer than she expected. As soon as she got into work, she booted up her computer and began looking at her calendar. She was supposed to be meeting with Susan to discuss suggestions for employee booster activities. She really hadn't thought of anything to do to boost employees and she really wished Susan hadn't asked her, but she was on point to come up with something. But all she could seem to focus on these days was having a baby. She looked at one of the sayings on her bulletin board. "But they that wait upon the LORD shall renew their strength; they shall mount up with wings as eagles; they shall run, and not be weary; and they shall walk, and not faint. Isaiah 40:31"

Giselle took a deep breath after reading the verse and relaxed her shoulders. She opened her email and there were at least ten red emails that she needed to read. She scanned the subjects and saw two messages from Susan. She clicked open the first message: *Giselle, no need to worry about employee boost activities. Our new employee Reyna brought some great suggestions and we are going to go with her ideas. Thanks anyway for taking on the task.*

"Oh okay then," Giselle said slowly to herself. She felt a sense of relief for not having to deal with the employee boost assignment anymore. *So Reyna came up with something, huh?*

She clicked on the second email from Susan: *Giselle, can you work with Reyna on her ideas for Bring Your Child to Work Day. We need an email blast to send out to employees and I think you can help her come up with the marketing design and copy text for the email. Thanks. Susan.*

"Bring Your Child to Work Day," Giselle exclaimed. "Now why would they choose something like that to boost employee morale. Everybody here doesn't have a child." Giselle thought about the small publishing office she worked for. It was mainly made up of women and there were only three men on the entire staff of 20. She thought about every woman there and when she realized that everybody had a child except her, she closed her eyes to stave off the tears that were forming. *Why would they want to do this?* Her morale certainly wasn't going to be boosted. She needed to talk to Reyna and quick. Plus, since Reyna had been a recent guest at her home, she wanted to get to know her a little bit better. She collected herself and walked over to Reyna's office.

"Hi, Giselle, I was waiting on you to come by. Sorry we had to leave the party so soon, but I had to tend to my son. Speaking of, did you hear that Susan liked my idea and we are going to have Bring Your Child to Work Day?

"I know we're going to send out a formal email, but I have spoken with a few of the ladies here and they are ecstatic. Isn't this exciting? It's going to be great to have our kids here together. I was telling Susan that we could plan some activities around the whole day to include lunch and…"

Giselle cut her off. "Reyna, it's a great idea, but you probably didn't know this when you suggested it, but as you know from the party, I don't have any children. I mean we are working on having a baby, but we've been unsuccessful so far." As fierce as she looked in her navy blue and pinstripe suit, her face said everything but fierce. She sincerely hoped that Reyna would understand.

"Oh girl, I didn't even think about that. But Giselle, you are the only one, so you think we should just come up with something else because you're the only one that can't actually participate?"

"No, I am not saying that. It's just that...never mind, Reyna. Just let me know what activities you want to do and we can work on the email today so that we can get it out by end of day. I will be in my cubicle if you need me."

"Okay girl." Reyna beamed. She wasn't letting up on her phony excitement at all. "I'll call you when I am ready. Give me about an hour to come up with the activities. K?"

"Yeah, okay," Giselle responded dryly. She walked away and bumped into her coworker friend Chaka.

"Giselle, why are you looking like you just lost your best friend?"

"Girl, you must not have heard."

"Heard what?"

"We're having Bring Your Child to Work Day."

Chaka frowned and pulled her neck back in confusion. "What? Who came up with that dumb idea? Shucks, that's why I come to work to get away from bad behind Mario." She laughed, but quickly cut it off when she noticed Giselle's face still looking sad.

"Awe dang, Giselle, I just thought about it. Girl, it's all right. You can act like Mario is your son and I will just act like I don't have a kid, okay."

Giselle pursed her lips. "Girl, it's all good. Reyna came up with this idea and if I had a kid I would probably be all excited like she is about the whole thing."

"Reyna came up with it. Humph. For some reason, I just don't like that female. I get a bad vibe when she comes around and you know my folks from New Orleans. I know how to detect that kind of stuff. And plus, she ain't the nicest person you know. Every time I speak to that heifer or see her in the kitchenette or the restroom, she never speaks first. I always have to speak to her. I'm stopping that though. She thinks *she* all special? I'm not catering to her behind no mo'."

"Chaka, that's not nice," Giselle scolded in a motherly tone. "But check this out. Reyna was at my house for the BBQ."

"What? How did that mean old heif-, okay, I mean, how did that *lady* end up at your crib?"

"Well check this out…she's a twin and her twin sister ReRe and my husband Remi went to high school together and are good friends, but nobody knew about her because she grew up in Louisiana with her grandma. Ain't that something?"

"Yeah that's something all right. That only means one thing when you have to go live with your grandma. You so dang gone bad, your parents can't handle your butt. See I know because I lived with my grandma and that was the exact reason why," she stated as a matter of fact.

Giselle laughed. "Well anyway, that's the deal, but I will be all right though, Chaka. God will bring us a baby soon enough. Probably not soon enough for this Bring Your Child to Work Day, but soon and very soon," she said with a slight smile.

"Giselle, girl, you are so country. I know that old church song. *Soon and very soon, we are going to see the King*," she sang while they shared a laugh.

Reyna silently joined in on the laughter, too. She had heard the entire conversation. *Soon and very soon, you're going to learn about your husband's child.*

⋙   ⋙   ⋙

Being the wife of real estate mogul Rohan Aguilar had its privileges. Charlotta had the luxury of being able to workout in the mornings before having a chef-prepared breakfast. She'd just finished her daily run at Memorial Park when she realized that she needed to get going on finding out more information about little miss Reyna. She had been thinking about how she was going to go about it.

"I could call my friend Missy Turner. If Missy doesn't know the information or how to find the information, the information isn't meant to be found," she said, while cutting into her five cheese omelet. "Maybe I can do a little online searching. I need to find out all I can on this Reyna Reynolds." She booted up her laptop and inserted her wireless card.

As a realtor's wife, the first place she went to start her search was the appraisal district to see if Reyna owned anything or had any homes in her name. She typed Reyna's name in the search. Nothing.

Next she did a Google search. Several blogs and Facebook matches came up and she saved a few of the sites to her favorites so that she could go back and look later. Charlotta continued to scroll down the list. She hit next page and quickly scanned the headlines. New Resident violates homeowners' association rules. Charlotta frowned up her nose when she noticed that the headline was from a River Oaks Community Newsletter. *She can't possibly afford to live in River Oaks, can she?* She clicked on the link to open up the newsletter. A PDF began to open. The newsletter was dated four years ago. She started reading the article.

THE VIOLATION HEARING FOR ASHBY LANE RESIDENT, REYNA REYNOLDS WILL BE HELD ON THURSDAY. REYNOLDS IS CHARGED WITH OVERGROWN DRIVEWAY WEEDS. WHEN ASKED BY THE RIVER OAKS COMMUNITY NEWS WHY SHE HAD NOT REMOVED THE WEEDS AFTER SEVERAL VIOLATION NOTICES, REYNOLDS RESPONDED: "I ONLY LIVE HERE. I DON'T PAY RENT OR DEAL WITH LANDSCAPING TYPE STUFF. YOU NEED TO TALK TO THE ACTUAL OWNER OF THE PROPERTY." AFTER SEVERAL SEARCHES, OUR STAFF CONTACTED R.A. REAL ESTATE HOLDINGS, THE OWNER OF THE PROPERTY ON ASHBY LANE.

Charlotta could not believe what she was reading. How could she not have known about any of this? R.A. Real Estate Holdings was one of her husband's real estate companies. She did a search for the house on the Harris County Appraisal District. There it was right there on the screen. Her husband was the owner of Reyna's house. But why or how in the world could that be, she wondered.

She then went back to the blogs she originally found. She needed to know a little bit more personal information about Reyna. Why was Rohan basically allowing her to live rent-free in this house and why didn't she know anything about it?

After clicking and searching around on the blog sites, the only thing she found was herself even more angry than before. She started thinking about Rohan cheating on her with Reyna and nearly lost her cool. She calmed herself as she stared at the screen with squinted eyes.

Contemplating. Thinking. Analyzing. Fuming. All were the emotions that she displayed. She pushed her half eaten omelet aside. She popped her neck and tried to relax her shoulders. She could feel the tension building.

"Okay Charlotta, why would Rohan cheat? It's not like you don't have the body and beauty of a twenty-something," she said. "Plus your marriage is solid."

After a few moments, Charlotta decided to forego trying to hatch up a secret plan to figure out what was going on. "I'm just going to call him. We've been married more than 25 years and have a grown son. I am not going to sit here and act like a kid in high school who thinks her boyfriend is cheating. Lord, give me the strength to handle whatever it is that I am about to find out."

She dialed Rohan's cell phone and nervously waited for him to pick up.

"Hola, mami!" Rohan answered. "How's my girl?"

Charlotta paused. She normally smiled when she talked to her husband for the first time of the day since they left each other's side in the bed, but this time she wanted to get straight to the point.

"Rohan, why are you paying for Reyna Reynolds to live on Ashby Lane in one of *our* houses? And please just the truth. No mess."

Rohan took a deep breath. He wanted to utter the three word phrase he knew so familiar from the 1970's show *Good Times*, when Florida Evans found out that her husband James had died, but he refrained from cursing.

"Mami, I can explain. But I don't want to do it right now. We can talk when I get home. Remi is about to come in here and meet with me on the Katy project."

Not wanting to accept his response, Charlotta paused before speaking. "I need to know something and soon, Rohan. I don't think this can wait until you get home. You are paying for a young woman to live in one of our homes. That deserves a right now explanation. I don't care about you and Remi's meeting. Your meeting with our son can wait. I am your wife and this is serious business."

"Charlotta, let me first just say that I understand where you are coming from and I want to put it out there that you have nothing to worry about when it comes to my love for you or our marriage. Everything is still as good as it was when I left this morning. What I need to tell you is very detailed and I don't want to talk about it here at work. Plus it has to do with Remi and I don't want him overhearing by mistake."

"What? What do you mean it has to do with Remi? Reyna? The house? What Rohan? Is everything all right with my baby boy?"

"Yes, honey. Remi is fine. But again, we're going to have to postpone this. So how was your run today, honey?" he asked, quickly changing the subject because Remi was at his door waiting for his dad to usher him in with a hand gesture.

Charlotta picked up on his change of tone. "Fine, Rohan. No working late tonight. Come home as soon as you can."

"That's great, baby. Okay, well Remi just walked in and we Aguilar men have some real estate business to tend to."

"Tell Remi Mommy says hi," she requested.

"Remi, your mother says hi. All right, honey. I will talk to you later. I love you, I love you, and you know I love you."

It was the familiar phrase that he had said to Charlotta when he first told her he loved her years ago. Remi smiled at him because it had been something he had heard his father tell his mother all his life. He admired their relationship and desired for he and Giselle to be like them when they were older.

"Hey Remi, come on in. Let's get down to work."

"So what's Mom up to? You two love birds planning something for tonight?"

"Oh, uh, naw, son. Just our usual daily chit chat. That's all. Now look, here are the plans that I wanted to talk to you about with the Katy project."

Remi noticed his father's odd and semi-nervous demeanor. He wanted to probe a little bit more, but he knew that his father wouldn't involve him in anything that wasn't his business. And by the looks of things, whatever he and his mother had just discussed wasn't any of his business.

Chapter 15

Jackie waited for Darnell to arrive at her house. After their chat last night, she hardly got any sleep. She paced the floor back and forth until she heard his truck pull into her driveway. She peered out her front window through the wooden blinds and saw him rushing to get out of the truck. She ran to the door and opened it just as he arrived at the door.

"Baby, please…just let me explain everything," he said as soon as he saw her face. She had the meanest look he had ever seen Jackie sport. Her nose was sprouted out like a mad bull and she looked like she wanted to just punch Darnell in his grill.

"Oh I plan to let you explain, Darnell, so start talking."

Darnell sat on her sofa and grabbed her hands. She snatched them away. How could he want to hold her hand after he had just told her that he was already married to someone else? Until she heard the reasoning behind his lies, she wasn't up for the chummy.

"Baby, you know I love you more than anything, right? I mean we just prayed to God and everything, right?"

"Darnell, I promise you, if you don't tell me what the deal is soon, I am going to lose it on you," she screamed.

"Okay, okay. Here goes…"

Darnell told Jackie the entire story about Maria and the latest call he had received from her. Not expecting Jackie to even remotely understand why he did what he did, Darnell watched as she kept silent throughout the story. She didn't know what to say and Jackie was known for always having something to say.

"I need you to stand by me while I handle this business, Jackie. Please, baby. Can you do that?" he asked in more of a begging tone.

"Lord have mercy on your soul, man. What have you done, Darnell? I mean, this is just a lot to digest."

"I know, but maybe we can talk to Pastor about it at our next session. In the meantime, the first thing I am going to do tomorrow is file for divorce from Maria. I think she will be fine, even though she doesn't seem to think so."

"Darnell, there is no way for us to get married if you are already married, so yes, your first priority is to get unmarried. I just can't believe this is happening to me. Lord why?"

"Baby, we prayed to a God that can fix anything, so we have to exercise our faith and trust Him at this point. I know I messed up and now I got you in my mess, but I promise to clean it up before you walk your beautiful self down that aisle."

He grabbed her hand again and this time she didn't remove it.

"You had better get it worked out, Darnell."

"I trust God to work it out. I know I messed up, but I know God can fix any mess we put ourselves in."

"Yes dear, that He can do. As long as we turn it over to Him, He can fix it."

The two held hands and put their foreheads together and closed their eyes.

"Help us, Lord. Help us to be what you want us to be, not our past. Help us to move forward to reach our ultimate goal of marriage, a marriage ordained by you Father. Amen."

"Amen, baby," Jackie replied. There was one thing she loved and that was a man who knew how to get one up to God himself.

❧   ❧   ❧

Faith reflected on the previous day. She was at work sitting in her office about to have another meeting on the changes that needed to be made to the ad campaign for Shay Praise. She pulled her journal out of her bag and began to write.

Dear Journal,

Yesterday was simply crazy. Gavin asked me to marry him. All those years that I longed to hear those words from him, he said it yesterday to get me to come back to him. How are we going to go from not even dating to engaged? I am just so glad that I didn't let that spirit of back and forth get into my head. I messed up and called him baby, because I got caught up in the moment.

It's like, I know that he is simply not the one God wants me to be with. God didn't remove me from that situation for nothing. He didn't make it where Chrishawn would be in the same place I am for nothing. All of this with Gavin was just a test to see if I would stick to the plan and purpose God has for my life. I do care a lot about Chrishawn and now that I am moving on and letting go of my past, I can finally focus on what God truly does have for me.

I pray for Gavin that God will give him someone who he can love and that they both love the Lord first. But enough about Gavin, my focus is now on the one that almost got away from me. Mr. Chrishawn Jackson. It's funny how things work out. I never would have guessed that I would be seriously involved with my best friend's brother. All those years growing up, I never would have thought it. He just didn't seem to be my type.

I know Chrissy and I aren't like we used to be, but maybe this step forward will rekindle our friendship. It won't be like it was before, but Chrissy has been my friend for a long time and we truly have a bond. I know she messed up big time, but it's really time for me to move away from that area of pain. I've felt it long enough. I release it in the name of Jesus.

Faith closed her journal and smiled. She felt a sheer sense of relief in her soul. She closed her eyes and took a deep breath. Before she could take another, Ana walked in.

"Hey, Faith, you okay, girlfriend?"

"Oh yeah, I am just breathing freshness into my life. What's going on, Ana?"

"I just wanted to come and tell you that I am leaving the company," she said with a nervous smile.

"What? Where are you going? When did this come about?"

"I just realized that if I want to move up in my career, I gotta take some risks. I've been waiting on these people to see my value and they haven't seen it yet. Plus, after you didn't make any recommendations for me to be your assistant, I thought long and hard about how I am portrayed here. Instead of me standing on my work, I wanted you to hook me up. That wasn't right and I am glad you didn't put your neck on the line for me."

"Ana, wait. I didn't recommend you because I haven't recommended anyone yet. I've been sort of consumed with my personal business and I really haven't had the opportunity to even talk to you about the job and what your goals are."

"Really, Faith?"

"Yes, Ana. I mean, you are right about me being turned off with your wanting a 'girlfriend hook up,' but I was actually going to just chat with you about what you really want from your career."

"Wow, Faith. I didn't know that. I'm glad to know that you didn't give up on me totally. But I have already turned in my notice. I am actually going to go back to school to become a speech language pathologist. I found this great program that will allow me to work in the field while I am in school. I love children and I think, make that I know, it's what I am meant to be doing. I am going to leave this advertising stuff up to you ad geeks." She laughed.

"Speech language, huh? That sounds like a great field, Ana. I am sure you will do well in it."

"I hope so. I am nervous about it, but it's time for me to stop waiting on other folks and take charge of my life. I hope we can stay in touch after I leave."

"Of course we can, Ana."

Ana went behind Faith's desk and surprised her with a hug. Faith was caught off guard, but welcomed the friendly side of Ana. This was a side that she had never really seen from her, but it felt totally genuine…like a breath of fresh air.

"I wish you the best here, Faith. You are very talented and that's why you scored that big account. I know you will continue to do well. And don't forget to invite me to you and Chrishawn's wedding."

That statement caught Faith more off guard than Ana's hug.

"Girl, can I just date the man first before you go marrying us off already." Faith laughed.

"Faith, that man is your husband. Watch what I tell you."

"All right Miss Psychic, are you sure you are not going into *that* field?"

They shared a laugh and Ana left Faith with the thought of marrying Chrishawn. She smiled at the thought, and then waved it off. *Let me just focus on dating the man first.*

❧   ❧   ❧

Gavin was back in Jackson. His father was back in Georgia and his grandfather was flying to Georgia to live with his dad in the next couple of days. Gavin's trip to California had not gone as planned with Faith, but he was glad that at least his family tree was firmly planted and on the mend. His sister Gavanna was thrilled to hear that she would be reconnecting with her father and grandfather. His mother was overcome with tears when she spoke to her ex-husband after Gavin had called his mom while they were at the hotel in California.

Gavin sat on his couch and went through all of his mail while sipping on a soda. He noticed that he had two envelopes. One was from Meharry Medical College and the other one was from the University of California, San Francisco. He had applied to both schools. Meharry because it was a black college and UC-San Francisco because Faith was there. He didn't know which one to open first. Not having relied on his faith since his Faith left Jackson, Gavin decided to pray. *Lord, if its meant for me to continue to pursue Faith, let this be an acceptance letter from UC. If I am to leave Faith alone and move forward with my life, let me get an acceptance letter from Meharry. And Lord, before all of that, let me please at least be accepted period to one of these schools. Amen.*

He tore open the letter from Meharry first. He scanned it. He had been accepted to Meharry with a full scholarship offer. His heart raced. He was so excited about the scholarship offer that he kept reading the letter to get the details. *Oh my God, you are so awesome. This is a sweet deal!*

Gavin was getting a full ride to Meharry with a yearly stipend. Unless UC offered all of that, Meharry was the better deal. He took a breath and slid his finger along the envelope to open the letter from UC. As soon as he saw the word *regret*, he knew that he had not been accepted. He read the letter in its entirety. It felt like he was reading a letter from the Lord telling him to move forward.

We regret to inform you that your application for admission was not accepted. UC would like to thank you for applying and while we were unable to grant you admission at our university, we hope that you will move forward with your plans to pursue a career in medicine. We wish you much success in your future endeavors.

Gavin took a five minute break to thank God for answering Him with certainty. He knew what he had to do now, and that was get ready to move to Nashville, Tennessee for the next chapter in his life. He was going to Meharry Medical College. He was going to be a physician. He called his mother and sister to share the news.

᥆ᥩ   ᥆ᥩ   ᥆ᥩ

Faith flopped down in her office chair. Her meeting had gone extremely well and she was on cloud nine. She absolutely loved her job. She noticed the red voicemail button illuminated on her phone. She had a message. She dialed the automated system to retrieve her messages.

"Hey Faith, it's Chrishawn. I hope we can spend some time together after you get off work. Call me when you get a chance."

Faith smiled at the thought of spending a little quality time with Chrishawn. She dialed his cell number.

"Of course we can spend some time together," she said as soon as he picked up the phone.

Chrishawn was grinning from ear to ear. "Okay, now that's what I am talking about. How about I meet you at your place and we can cook some stir fry together."

"Oh yeah, that sounds good. I'll pick up the stuff on my way home."

"No need, I got everything we need."

Faith thought about that. She was silent so long Chrishawn had to call her name to break her out of her train of thought.

"I'm here, Chrishawn. And I mean that in more ways than one. I am really here this time. We can chat tonight, but I just want you to know that I am really here."

"I'm glad, Faith. I'm so glad you are really here…with me."

Faith hung up from Chrishawn and checked her email. She needed to work with Malik on a few more designs before she called it a day.

She maneuvered through all the emails until she saw the last one that had come in. The name was in red. GAVIN ROBERTS.

She thought about not opening it. Just when she was ready to move on, he had emailed her. She prayed a quick prayer. *Lord, let this be something good. Let this be Gavin moving on.*

She began to read the email:

Hey Faith, just wanted to let you know my good news. I got accepted at Meharry Medical College! I am so excited, girl, you just don't know. I knew you would want to know since you helped me stay on track so many times back at Jackson State. I can't even begin to tell you how excited I am. Paging Dr. Roberts, here I come! LOL. Well, anyway, I am sure you are busy with your big account over there, so I won't take up too much of your time.

But I will say this: Thank you for everything you have ever done for me. Thank you for showing me Christ. Thank you for helping me mend my relationship with my father and grandfather. Thank you for putting up with me when I tried to win you back. Faith, I got two letters in the mail while I was there in California. While I was trying to get you back, God already had His plan worked out for me. I prayed before I opened the letters. I prayed that if I was to continue trying to get you back for me to get accepted to UC San Francisco. If I was to move forward and let you go, to get accepted to Meharry.

Well you already know how God answered it. The funny and weird part is I have peace about it. I didn't expect that, but I remember some verse in the Bible about God giving you peace that surpasses all understanding. That is truer in my life right now than ever. I don't understand it, but I accept this peace that I have about us. I wish you all the success in the world, Faith. I do still love you because even with peace, my heart still has love for you and probably always will. But I know that I must move forward with my life. Again, thanks for everything. I hope that we can at least keep in touch in the future. Love, Gavin

Faith felt a tear drop down her right cheek. It was finished. It was really over this time and she felt that same freshness she had felt earlier. She called her aunt Jackie to fill her in on the final saga.

Faith delved right into the conversation after he aunt picked up the phone. When she noticed that her aunt wasn't responding in her usual way, Faith stopped talking to see what was going on.

"Aunt Jackie, are you okay? You haven't said a word and I have been going on and on."

"Faith, I just have a lot going on right now, sweetie. I am glad to hear that everything is working out on your end and that you are moving on with Chrishawn and Gavin is moving on with his life."

"What's going on with you? I hope you are not stressing about this wedding stuff. I have my dress, shoes, jewelry and everything I need. I have already asked to be off those days and I already got my flight in order to arrive early so that I can help you out."

Jackie took a deep breath. She didn't know if she should share Darnell's business with anyone, especially since what he had done was illegal.

"So are you going to tell me what's going on with you?" Faith questioned.

"Faith, it's best that I don't talk about it, honey. Just pray for me and Darnell that everything will work out the way God intends it to work out."

"Whoa, wait a minute. Is the wedding up in the air? What's going on, for real now? You got me worried over here. Y'all are my flesh and blood, so I think it's okay to tell me."

Jackie proceeded to tell Faith about Darnell's marriage to Maria and how she hoped everything could be finalized before the wedding in the next couple of weeks.

"Aunt Jackie, look. Let's just pray about it and leave it to God. That's what you always taught me. So just pray and let God fight this battle. Where is Darn...I mean Dad now anyway?"

"He's trying to get everything taken care of. I sure hope he does in time. I'm ready to be his wife and I have a wedding planned, venues reserved, vendors working on favors and everything. I mean, I can cancel all that, but I just want it to work out, you know."

"I know. I know. Me too. And it will. The wedding will take place. No need to worry."

Chapter 16

Giselle came home and fell out on the sofa. She was tired. Reyna had worked her nerves so bad that she was starting to think the girl had something against her. *Lord, why do I have to deal with this? I want a baby, Lord. I want to be able to participate in Bring Your Child to Work Day.* Giselle started crying uncontrollably. The more she thought about Reyna, the more her faith decreased.

Remi walked in and saw his wife asleep on the couch. He noticed all of the used tissues strewn about the floor and on the sofa. He knew she had been crying. And he knew why. He too wanted so badly for them to get pregnant. He wanted his wife to feel some relief from the burden she had placed on herself for trying so hard to get pregnant. Remi startled Giselle when he reached beside her to pick up the used tissues.

"Oh, Remi, you scared me."

"I'm sorry, baby. I was just trying to clean up these tissues. You okay, G? What's wrong with my baby?"

The word baby just made her start crying all over again. She fell into Remi's chest and started rambling about her work day and bringing a child to work. All Remi heard was Reyna and it made him think about his encounter with ReRe.

After a few moments of tears, Giselle left Remi and went to lie down in their bed. She told him she didn't want to talk anymore. Remi hated the way this was weighing on her. But the more he thought about Reyna, the more he thought about ReRe. He needed to call her to settle the thoughts that permeated his mind.

He decided to leave the house and go outside to call her. He didn't want Giselle to hear his conversation. He dialed her number from the caller ID.

"Hello."

"ReRe, this is Remi. How you doing, girl?"

"Oh hey there, Remi. What's up with you?"

"Oh nothing much, just giving you a call since we didn't really get a chance to talk much at the BBQ."

"Yeah, I'm sorry we had to leave the other day. My sister is…" she paused before she stated how crazy her sister was. ReRe was a Christian and she believed that verse in the bible that says as a man thinketh, so is he. She didn't want to think about her sister being crazy because to her, thinking it might just make it true. "My sister was very concerned about her son, so we had to leave."

"Oh it's all good. You guys just missed out on some of my best BBQ that's all." He laughed. Remi and ReRe talked for another few minutes before he decided to bring up the spring break incident.

"So ReRe, before today, we haven't seen each other since spring break my freshman year. Remember the club?"

"What club, Remi? Freshman year was a while ago, but I don't remember any clubs. You know I'm not really the club type anyway." She smiled.

"I saw you at the mall that day and we met up at the club. Please tell me that you remember that night." Remi was starting to wonder how ReRe could forget such a memorable night; at least it was very memorable to him.

"Nope, you got me, Remi. I don't remember any club or you being home. The last time I saw you was at our high school graduation party, I believe."

Remi started running the memory through his mind. Everything had been so strange about that night, but he had just chalked it up to ReRe letting loose since high school.

"Wait a minute. My sister was living in Houston at that time. Maybe you mistakenly thought she was me. Did she act like she was me? Because when she got here, she did some crazy stuff trying to get back at me and my parents for her not being raised with the family. She pretended to be me a lot to sabotage my reputation. I had to deal with a lot of stuff back then. It was nuts."

"Oh my goodness, ReRe! I had no idea it wasn't you. I thought it was strange how you came on to me at the mall and the way you danced with me at the club."

"What? Now Remi, you've known me well enough to know I would never come on to you in any sort of provocative way. That should have been your first clue that you weren't dealing with me."

"Seriously ReRe, you two look so much alike and with me not knowing you even had a twin sister, how was I not supposed to assume that you hadn't totally changed since we left high school?"

"Well, well, my sister Reyna strikes again. So you want to tell me what happened that night so that I can at least know what you know."

"It's pretty crazy, ReRe, and now that I know it wasn't you, I feel like total crap right now for getting fooled by your sister. I mean we...."

"You what?"

"ReRe, I don't know how to say this, but we...I mean I thought it was you."

"What are you saying, Remi? What happened that night?"

"Oh my God, I can't believe this is happening. This is like something straight out of a crazy movie," he said while pacing the perimeter of their swimming pool.

"Remi, are you going to tell me or just talk around it? Get to it. What happened with my sister?"

He paused, looked back at the house to make sure Giselle wasn't looking out of a window. He contemplated holding in the secret. But he just couldn't. He spilled it fast.

"We had sex in the back of my dad's truck at the club that night. And I thought it was you though, ReRe, honest. I just thought you had finally come around and we had been drinking shots and you just, I mean your sister, UGH!" Remi said obviously frustrated.

"What! You had sex with my sister, Remi? Oh my goodness, this is definitely the straw that broke the camel's back with that sister of mine. She is a conniving, evil spirit who needs Jesus for real. I cannot believe she would stoop so low and get you to believe that she was me and then go as far as having sex with you."

"ReRe, I am so sorry. I really thought it was you and I thought I was lucky. But just like my wife told me when we were dating, sex screws everything up when you are not married. Dang, man how could I have been so stupid?" he fumed.

"You were just being a young man, Remi. A stupid young man, but it was your raging hormones. My sister is the one that is the trickster. And I know she knew what she was doing. Everything she has done to try to hurt me and my parents has been crazy, but this one just takes the cake. You know the only thing good that has come from her crazy behind is her son Recio. I love him so much. He may have come from my sister's womb, but he doesn't seem to have inherited her craziness."

"Yeah children are definitely a gift from God. Me and my wife are trying to have a baby ourselves, but we haven't been fortunate to hear the great news from the doctors yet. We've been trying though and truth be told, as much as I enjoy the trying part, I am ready to hear those words."

"Well, you guys just have to keep the faith, Remi. Like you said, children are a gift from God. I know that if God blessed my sister with a baby, you are definitely on his list to get one," she smiled. "Reyna doesn't even know who Recio's father is or at least she won't tell us. But with you two being married, God will honor your covenant with him and bless you with a child soon."

"Thanks, ReRe. Your words are like music to my ears. Speaking of music, you still playing your clarinet." He laughed at the thought.

"Boy, please. I put that thing on the shelf as soon as we graduated high school. You miss marching in that Sonic Boom at Jackson State?"

"Man, do I. I love that band. It was so awesome. You would have loved playing in the band there. We went on so many trips and played in so many different venues. It was really a blast to be a part of such a historic band. Those of us band alumni will always Luv Da Boom," he said proudly. "Well look, I just stepped outside to holla at you for a minute. I need to get back in the house before Giselle comes looking for me. But ReRe?"

"Yeah, Remi," she replied.

"I don't know how to say this, but I am really sorry about the incident with your sister. You have to know that I would never do that to a friend like you. I honestly thought it was you."

"Remi, you don't have to apologize. That was years ago and we have all grown up since then. Well at least you and I have. I don't even know if I will bring this up to my sister. The bible says to forget those things in the past and press on toward the future, so I think I will follow the good book and just let it go. Promise me you won't beat yourself up about it. I mean sex is a big deal, but God forgives all sin."

"You are right, ReRe. And I know God has forgiven me for all of my sins because that is my prayer every night. It's funny, but now everything is starting to make sense. After that incident, I wondered why we never talked. But anyway, thanks for forgiving me. You're still that sweet wholesome girl I know."

"I have done my dirt, too, Remi, so I am not all that wholesome, but what I am, is a sinner saved by God's grace. Without God, I wouldn't be anywhere."

"Amen to that. My wife is the one who brought me into the true fold of Christ. She's my heart and I love her so much. That's why I pray that God blesses us with a child soon."

"I pray God's will for your lives, too, Remi. Have a good one okay and don't be a stranger."

"I won't, ReRe. You take care."

Remi hung up the phone and stood by the pool. He could see his reflection. He thought about his conversation with ReRe. He couldn't believe that he had been bamboozled by Reyna. As much as he tried to fight the urge, he wanted to confront her about it. *I know that ReRe said it was the past, but Reyna and I need to talk about this. I can't just go on, knowing that she fooled me and I slept with her. I need to talk to her myself.*

ReRe hung up the phone from Remi. Her sister had stooped to a new low with this new information she had just learned. She told Remi that she wasn't going to say anything and she wasn't, but she prayed to God that He would forgive her sister's tirades. ReRe knew that her sister would have to come to God for herself and ask for forgiveness, but as her twin, she felt she could at least get the ball rolling.

As ReRe contemplated the story that Remi revealed, she shot up in her bed when she thought about her nephew Recio, and Reyna not revealing his father. Could Remi be Recio's father? She calculated the math in her head from Reyna's pregnancy and when Remi said they had sex. "OH MY GOD! Remi. Reyna. Recio. Could it be?"

Remi went back inside and grabbed a bottled water. As he gulped the water down, he thought about his conversation with ReRe. He felt bad on the inside, but he kept reminding himself it was just a big mistake from his past. *I know how to deal with this. I am just going to call Reyna at her job tomorrow and tell her to meet me somewhere. We have to talk about this. I need closure on this new revelation.*

∽   ∽   ∽

After Rohan explained everything to his wife, all Charlotta could do was sit there in silence. She couldn't believe Reyna had been blackmailing Rohan all this time and she didn't have a clue. Being mad and angry at her husband for keeping this from her was not even close to the emotions she felt knowing that she had a grandson out there and had not been part of his life.

"So have you spent any time with the little boy?" she said breaking her silence.

"No, Charlotta. I have just tried to keep this crazy girl from ruining our son's life. She is a psycho, honey, I am telling you. If you only knew all the stuff she has tried to do to ruin Remi, you wouldn't be thinking about that little boy."

"That little boy is our grandson, Rohan. How can you be so insensitive? A child is involved. This isn't just a situation where Remi slept with a girl, but he impregnated this girl and she had a baby, our son's baby, our grandson."

"Honey, I understand because you are new to this whole deal, but she's evil. And I haven't thought much about Recio other than making sure he has everything he needs monetarily. I don't really want to have a relationship with Reyna Reynolds."

"Rohan!" Charlotta screamed. "It's not about that girl. It's about our grandson. If she is as evil as you say she is, then we need to rescue our grandson from her. I think you are just too focused on Remi's career to even see the enormity of this situation. We have a grandson, Rohan, our flesh and blood. Clearly you have not seen him enough to feel anything for the little boy, huh?"

"I've seen him, Charlotta, but I don't feel anything but disdain when I see her."

"For the love of God, it's not about her. It's about the baby. I want to see him. I want to talk to Reyna. I need to get involved in this mess to get it resolved."

Rohan rubbed his temples. His signature move when he felt overwhelmed. He thought he had kept this situation handled. The last thing he wanted to do was make matters worse getting his wife involved.

"Why are you even looking worried, Rohan? We are going to get this mess resolved and not by paying that girl anymore money. She's going to find her own place to live. The gravy train stops here. If she wants the baby taken care of, we will do it."

"What about Remi? How are we going to explain this to him?"

"We? We, Rohan? You are the one who made the situation worse than what it was by keeping it a secret. *You* are going to just be an adult and tell your adult son. I will be right there to support you and my son, but *you* are going to talk to him."

"What about, Giselle? Have you thought about how this is going to affect her?"

"Have you thought about how it could affect her if she finds out from somebody else that her husband has a son out there? Get a grip, Rohan. The jig is up. Reyna Reynolds will no longer control the Aguilar family."

Rohan admired the strength of his wife. He had always heard the stereotypes about African-American women, and he was married to a strong black woman.

"Baby, I love you so much. I am glad that you aren't mad at me for keeping this from you."

"Oh, don't get it twisted, baby, I am furious at you for keeping this from me, but right now, I am focused on getting the issue resolved, not fueling it with my anger."

"I understand," Rohan replied somberly. "I want you to know that I have never kept anything else from you. To be honest, I wanted to tell you, but this whole situation just got out of hand. I thought I could just throw money on it to make it go away."

"You should know you can't throw money on a fire, sweetheart. All it will do is burn. Let's just move forward and get this worked out the best way possible."

Chapter 17

"So you're really going to come home with me, Armando?" Chrissy asked with a giddy, child-like tone. Armando had come by early so they could work out together before work.

"Yep, I'm going to the Sip with you, girl," he replied back with just as much excitement.

Chrissy and Armando had been inseparable since she got to New York. Outside of working, the two were stuck like glue. Chrissy was glad that God had blessed her to get Armando as her driver. Now he was becoming more than her driver; he was her friend.

"Well my friend's aunt is getting married on that Friday. Do you think we could leave out Thursday night to make the wedding?"

"I am not sure, sweetness," he said with his Puerto Rican accent. "We'll have to play it by ear since I may have to work. I can't promise you that we will get there in time for wedding, but we can definitely try."

"Okay," she hesitantly replied. She really wanted to make Jackie and Darnell's wedding, but as long as she got home for that weekend, she would be able to see everybody. Remi and Giselle were coming from Houston, and Chrishawn was coming home for the first time since he left for California.

"Well, let me call my brother and let him know that you are coming. I am so excited and I know my mother will have tons of questions, so I am going to wait and tell her." She laughed.

"Whatever you want to do, sweetness." He winked. Chrissy almost lost her mind when he revealed those deep dimples.

God, you are so good to me.

She dialed her brother's number. With the three-hour time differ-
ence, she knew he was going to be mad about her calling him so early,
but she had to share her news about Armando coming home with her.

Chrishawn wasn't up, but he was happy to hear from his sister.

"I knew that dude would be coming with you. I just had this feeling.
Every time I talk to you, he is there. I knew you wouldn't be leaving
him there for a minute. Y'all are really hitting it off, huh, lil sis?" he
said while rubbing the sleep from his eyes. He looked at the clock. It
was 4 a.m. pacific time.

"Yes, Chrishawn, it has been unbelievable how this has all happened
so fast. My job is good, I may have a potential boyfriend, and you and
Faith are finally on. All I need is to bring my baby girl up here to NYC
and everything will be perfect."

"Yeah, it sounds like things are working out for you, sis. I am really
happy for you. For a minute there, I didn't know what was going to
happen with you or with me when it came to our relationships. But
God."

"You're so right. But God. I think Gavin getting accepted to
Meharry really helped things move along. I wish him the best you
know."

"Gavin will be all right. Being in medical school will keep him
very busy. I know that he will miss Grace, but he's making the right
moves to set up a better life for Grace anyway. When he finishes with
med school, that boy is going to be paid, and that means Grace won't
want for nothing." He laughed.

"I know, right. But I am talking about wishing him the best on the
relationship front. Since he and Faith broke up and we tried our hand
at a courtship, he's not had the best of luck, you know."

"Well, God knows who's best for whom. You know what I'm
saying. Faith was meant for me. And who knows, Armando may be
the one for you. God will orchestrate everything according to his will

and things will always work out the way they are supposed to, even when things don't initially seem like they will. We have to always keep God first in everything we do."

"Preach it, big brother. You 'bout to get your preaching license, ain't ya?" She laughed.

"See while you over there playing, I am. God has done a new thing in me and I want to serve him for the rest of my life, and that includes working in his kingdom. I mean I already work as the youth director, but I want to get my masters degree in theology. When I finish up this bachelor's program, I plan to enroll in seminary school."

"Wow, Chrishawn. I never would have thought my big brother would be a minister."

"That's the thing, baby sis, when you surrender your life to Christ, you allow him to tell to you what to do and that's what he is calling me to do."

"Well all right then, Minister Jackson. I know you will do well. Are you still going to target the youth?"

"Fa sho. Don't get it twisted, ya boy is still a young stunner with plenty of swagger," he said and burst into laughter at his attempt to talk like the young kids he worked with daily.

Chrissy joined in the laughter. "You sound a mess, boy. Is that how the kids talk though? I guess I haven't been around any young folks lately."

The two continued their jovial conversation and made plans to spend some quality time together while home in Mississippi the following week.

∽ ∽ ∽

It was 7:30 in the morning and Rohan made the call. He told Reyna he needed to meet with her to discuss the house and a few other details about Recio's school payments. Reyna had agreed to meet him after work. Charlotta gave Rohan a nod of approval after he hung up from Reyna. It was time to handle business.

Remi was at the office early. He needed to find Reyna's contact info. He searched until he found her. There she was on Facebook. He first befriended ReRe on Facebook. He knew she would have Reyna as one of her friends.

He sent her a direct message: *Hey Reyna, it's Remi, your sister ReRe's friend from high school. I wanted to holla at you for a minute. Can I get your phone number or email or something? I need to talk to you.*

Remi waited for a response. He saw that she was online. A chat message popped up. It was Reyna. *What do you need to talk to me about, Remi?*

Remi thought about it for a minute before he replied. He didn't want to come out and say what he *really* wanted to talk to her about on Facebook, so he lied.   *I am trying to plan a surprise for my girl and I know you both work at the same place. I need your help.*

Oh okay, cool, she replied back. *Here is my info. Call me.*

Can we just meet somewhere so we can talk? I don't want Giselle to hear me talking to you and since you work with her, I don't want her to hear you talking to me.

Remi knew that was highly unlikely, but he had to get her off of Facebook for a real face to face meeting.

"*Okay, let's meet at Ra Sushi for lunch today.*

Remi really hadn't wanted to meet in such a popular place, but he didn't want to press the issue of where they would meet, so he agreed.

Reyna looked at a mirror on her desktop and smiled.

It's showtime, Reyna, she thought. *You've been waiting to reconnect with Remi since that night at the club. Just like that night, he won't be able to resist you.* She adjusted her red v-neck top so that her red lace bra would play peek-a-boo to anyone who dared to stare. Just as she was about to reapply her red lipstick, someone knocked at her office door.

"Oh, hey Giselle. What's up girlfriend?" she sung happily.

Giselle was caught off guard by her girlfriend reference. She didn't know what to say as Reyna batted her long jet black eyelashes at her, waiting for a response.

"I just came by to tell you that Susan has decided to postpone the employee activity of bringing your child to work. It seems that a few people wanted to know if they could bring their animals in verses their children and it caused a ruckus, so Susan wants to see if we can do something else that would be more inclusive like a team building exercise. I've done some preliminary research and Dave and Busters has this type of thing at their restaurant."

Giselle entered Reyna's office and placed the print outs about the team building on her desk. As Reyna closed her compact to look at the printout, she moved just enough for Giselle to see her computer screen. *Figures she's on Facebook and not working,* Giselle thought. Then Giselle noticed the familiar picture. It was her husband Remi. Why was he on her screen? *Don't freak out, Giselle. Just chill.*

"Okay, well this looks like fun, Giselle. Let's meet after lunch to discuss the particulars. I was really looking forward to "bring your child to work day". I had already told my son Recio that he would get a chance to come and see where Mommy works."

"That's nice," Giselle responded dryly. "You want to meet around two?" she asked, trying not to get pulled into a long drawn out conversation with Reyna about her son.

"That's cool. We can meet in the conference room near your desk if that's all right with you. I need to really clean my office up and when my office is crazy, my creative juices are stifled." She laughed more to herself than to Giselle.

"See you at two," Giselle said on her way out the door.

Giselle left Reyna's office in deep thought. She knew people were always reconnecting on Facebook, so she tried to shake the uneasy feeling she had about Reyna having Remi's page up. *Knowing her, she probably did that on purpose*, she surmised. *But how did she even know I was going to come into her office? Maybe she already knew Susan had postponed the activity and I would have to come in there and talk to her about it. Giselle, don't overanalyze this. You trust your husband, so you don't have anything to worry about.*

Reyna pulled her red beamer up to the valet at Ra Sushi restaurant. She exited the car and walked in to take the elevator to the second floor. Remi saw her when she pulled up. He was sitting in the open air patio portion of the restaurant. He had already figured out how he was going approach the subject…head on.

The hostess directed Reyna toward Remi's table and she tugged at her tight black skirt to make sure it was sitting just right on her. She saw the quick glimpses she got from a few of the male patrons and the I-hate-you stares from the women. This was the norm for her. With a classic and beautiful face like a young Vanessa Williams, she sashayed her way over to Remi's table

"Remi, how are you," she said in a seductive tone.

Remi cleared his throat and stood to pull out her chair. No matter how conniving she was, he was still going to be the gentleman that his mom had raised. "I'm good, Reyna. Glad we could meet on such short notice."

"Oh it's no problem. I'm glad I can help you surprise your wife. So what's this all about anyway? Is her birthday coming up or something?" she asked while taking a sip of the water the waitress had just placed in front of her.

"Reyna, to be honest, I brought you here because I wanted to confront you. Why did you pretend to be your sister that night at the club?"

Reyna nearly choked on her water. She wasn't expecting this from Remi at all. She cleared her throat and adjusted herself in her chair.

She retracted her neck inward and spoke. "Excuse me, Remi. I don't know what you speak of," she lied.

"Oh, you know very well, Reyna. I talked to ReRe and she said it was not her, so unless y'all have another sister, it was you that night. You fooled me into thinking that you were ReRe. Why would you do that?"

"Remi, I am just appalled at the accusations you are slinging across the table at me. Here I am thinking we are meeting to discuss your wife, and you are accusing me of sleeping with you at Club Roxy."

"See Reyna, I didn't even say what club. Why you playing me, girl? Haven't you done that enough? What's your problem anyway?"

"My problem," she said while placing her hand across her chest. "I don't have a problem, Remi. Don't blame me because you can't control your penis." She laughed devilishly. "You need to make sure you know who you are sleeping with before you go poking that thing around. If you weren't so horny that night, you might have known that I wasn't ReRe. "But if I recall correctly," she stated with furrowed eyebrows, "you thoroughly enjoyed yourself."

Remi was fuming on the inside. He wanted to snatch Reyna from her chair and throw her crazy self over the second floor patio balcony. How could she be so evil? ReRe said she was, but he didn't think she was this crazy.

"Look-a-here, Reyna," Remi said with a stern tone. But before he could finish, Reyna cut him off.

"No you look-a-here. I don't have time for this B.S. okay. I came here with good intentions and you are railroading me with old drama.

It happened and that's it. You don't have to worry about me wanting to sleep with you again, okay. You need to be focused on sleeping with your wife so that y'all can finally have a baby, so that pitiful heifer can stop whining around the office about not having a baby."

Before he knew what had happened, Remi grabbed Reyna's neck and started strangling her. The waiters and the waitresses tried their best to pull him off of her, but Reyna's red stilettos were dangling from the ground and she was gasping for air.

After a few more men came over, Remi finally let go and Reyna fell to the ground. Remi didn't know what got into him, but when Reyna talked about Giselle like that, he lost it.

"Somebody call the police on this fool. He tried to kill me," Reyna screamed. She was still on the ground trying to regain her composure.

Remi dashed out of the restaurant before the police arrived. He didn't need to ruin his stellar real estate reputation.

"Ma'am, do you need anything before the ambulance gets here?" the waitress asked.

"Ambulance? I don't need any ambulance. I need the police!" She nearly screamed at the waitress.

"I think someone called the police, too, ma'am."

"Good, I am pressing charges against that punk!"

As Remi dashed down Westheimer Road in his very noticeable Hummer with all the real estate stuff on it, he didn't know what to do or what to think. What if she decided to press charges against him? He kept replaying the scene in his head. He had never lost his cool like that with anyone. He prayed to God and called his father. If she did press charges, his father was well-known enough to get him out of it. He had to tell his dad what was going on.

"Dad…it's Remi. I might be in some trouble."

Chapter 18

Reyna called Susan at the office and told her that she'd had a situation and would not be able to return to work from lunch.

After getting a thorough check by the ambulance service and a clearance that nothing was physically wrong with her, she drove home. The police had asked her numerous times if she wanted to press charges, but she just couldn't do that to Remi. She loved him and he was Recio's father. She didn't want to make any trouble for him. *I've got a figure out a way to resolve this with my man.*

She walked into her walk-in closet and pushed back the long coats. There it was. Her shrine to Remi Aguilar. She had pictures of him in his college band uniform. She had pictures of him in his tuxedo at his and Giselle's wedding. She loved when he wore his khaki pants and real estate polo to work. She had more than 100 pictures of him in her closet.

Recio knew all about his father, too. She had told him stories about how his father was going to come and rescue them from living alone. Being a small child, Recio didn't really understand anything other than that was his daddy and he wanted to play with him.

Okay, Reyna, get it together, dear. You've made it this far with your plan. I know you weren't expecting Remi to reach out to you this early in the plan, but now you just have to adjust, okay. You've got Giselle where you want her by getting that job at Houston Heights. Remi's seen you looking your sexiest and his father...oh shoot, I am supposed to meet with my father-in-law this evening. Darn it.

Reyna pulled the clothes back in place to cover up her shrine. She needed to tidy up the house since Mr. Aguilar was stopping by in a few hours. With all that was going on, she had almost forgotten about his call. She needed to make sure she still had him wrapped around her finger.

"What was it he said he wanted to talk about anyway?" she said. "Whatever it is, I can handle it. I am Reyna Reynolds and people in this world better act like they know."

She went in the office and pulled out a wire notebook that had seen its better days. Her plan had been in motion ever since she found out she was carrying Remi's child. She reviewed her notes in the notebook. Everything had been going according to plan until today, but it would all be over very soon. She and Remi would finally be together so they could live as a family, something that she never had growing up.

I need my energy for when Mr. Aguilar shows up. Reyna went to her room and pulled out the framed picture of Remi in his tuxedo from her nightstand. She had cut Giselle's face out of the picture and put a picture of herself in the cut out spot. She kissed the frame and put it under her pillow. This was something she did every night.

恘 恘 恘

"Charlotta, I don't think it is wise for you to go over there with me. I can handle this, honey."

Rohan had stayed home from work trying to figure out his plan of attack for Reyna. After he got the call from Remi, he knew this was it. Reyna's shenanigans had to stop. Remi still didn't know about Recio. He was more worried about Reyna pressing charges. Rohan had assured him that everything would be fine and that he would go by and visit Reyna to work it out. Remi didn't even catch on to the fact his father knew where Reyna lived. Remi just didn't want Giselle to find out. His father promised him that he would take care of everything like always.

"I don't care what you say, Rohan. I am going over there with you. That girl is absolutely crazy and I am convinced of it. She works up there with Giselle, she got you wrapped around her pinky, and then she causes my son to lose his temper on her? Oh heck naw, I am going with you."

"Fine, Charlotta, but promise me you won't do anything crazy."

"Now that, I *cannot* promise. That girl better hope that the Jesus in me loves the Jesus in her…if He is even in her. When I get through with her though, she'll be calling on His name for sure!"

◅ ◅ ◅

It was after 2:00 and Giselle decided to leave the conference room. She bumped into Susan on her way out. "Hey Susan, have you seen Reyna? We were supposed to meet at 2:00 and she hasn't shown up yet."

"Well actually Reyna called in saying she couldn't come back from lunch. She'd had a situation at lunch and she needed to take the rest of the day off."

"Really? Do you know what happened?"

"She didn't give any details, but I am sure she will be back tomorrow and you guys can reschedule your meeting for then."

"Well, I need to reserve the space at Dave and Busters as soon as possible, so I was hoping that she and I could discuss a few things today so that I could get moving on this."

"I have her cell number. Let me get that for you. I don't think she would mind if you called her, especially since you need to make those reservations."

Giselle followed Susan back to the office to get Reyna's cell number. As much as she didn't want to call her, she needed to get those reservations made.

Giselle went back to her desk and made the call.

"Hello, Reyna?"

"Yes, who is this?"

"Hey, it's Giselle from work."

"What-do-you-want?" she asked with much attitude.

Giselle rolled her eyes and wished she had opted for not making the call.

"Look, Reyna, Susan gave me your number because I need to ask you a few things about this project so that I can make the reservations at Dave and Busters. That's all. You really need to check your tone.

"I don't know what it is about me that you don't like or what it is that makes you go back and forth on how you treat me, but it needs to stop right now. We are both grown women, and I deserve the same respect that you give everybody else."

"Giselle, honey, you don't deserve anything, okay." Reyna felt herself getting upset. She usually knew how to calm down her extreme temper flare-ups that she had been having since she was a child.

Reyna began to breathe hard and found herself holding her chest. She was having another episode. And then it happened.

"Look you stupid heifer, he is mine, okay. I don't have to give you any respect. I have respected your little narrow behind since he met you and married you, but he is mine. He is mine you hear me you Christian heifer. Forget that God talk you be talking. That's why you not pregnant because God didn't want you to be pregnant.

"He wanted me to be pregnant with Remi's baby and I was. I had his baby. He is mine and the baby is mine and we will be together forever. You are just so stupid. You don't even know that your husband has a baby almost four years old. How stupid can you be?

"Walking around the office whining and carrying on. Nobody cares about you, Giselle. Not me, not Remi, not nobody. You are just a stupid little girl from that hick state. Well you're in Houston now, trick, and you better act like you know up in this piece.

"This is Reyna's world and you have lived in it long enough. Consider yourself out! I bet you don't even know he met me for lunch. Sure we had a fight, but he still loves me, and I still love him. That's why I didn't press charges against him. I love Remi. And he's mine!" she hollered into the phone.

There was panting, breathing, chest holding, and then a loud scream. "UGH!" Reyna threw the phone against the wall and started throwing anything her hands could grab. *I hate that stupid heifer. I hate her. I hate her. I hate her. Where are my pills? Where the heck are my pills? I need to calm down. I need to calm down. 1-2-3. Forget that counting crap. I need my meds.*

When the phone line went dead, Giselle couldn't move. She didn't know what had just happened. She sat there for what seemed like an eternity before Susan came to her desk and broke her transient state.

"Giselle, did you talk to Reyna?"

Giselle still clutching the phone, looked at Susan and tried to speak but no words came out of her mouth.

"Giselle, are you okay? Who's on the phone? Did you just get some bad news or something?"

Giselle again tried to speak but nothing came out. She felt the tears flowing down her face.

"Oh my God, honey, what is it?" Susan probed as she took the phone. "Hello, is anybody there." There was no one on the phone so Susan hung it up.

"Giselle, please tell me what is it? Chaka, Chaka, can you come here please." Susan hollered over the cubicles. "Honey, I don't know what is wrong with Giselle. Do you know who she was just talking to? She hasn't said a word."

"I'm sorry, but I don't know. I just got back to my desk. Giselle, girl what's going on? You know you can talk to me."

"I gotta go, guys. I just gotta go," Giselle said as she grabbed her purse and ran in between the two ladies.

Giselle drove around the city until her fuel light came on. She didn't know who to call or what to do. She wanted to call Remi, but felt she couldn't. She didn't know how to explain what all had just gone down on the phone with Reyna.

She pulled her Ford Flex into the Shell station to get more gas. After she got her fill-up, she got back in the car and just sat there. Where would she go now? She heard a still small voice. *I am here. Talk to me.*

Oh Lord, she cried. *What is going on with my life right now? Who is this Reyna chick and why did she say all those things to me about Remi and her having a baby?* Giselle continued to cry her problems out to the Lord. She sat in the gas station lot until she heard a horn. She turned and looked at the window. A man was standing there smiling.

"Excuse me, miss, can you move forward if you have pumped your gas please, thanks." He walked back to his car.

Giselle only heard move forward. She put the key in the ignition and did exactly that. She moved forward, and the further she got away from the spot she had been sitting in, the more clearer her vision became. She needed to call her husband and God would take care of the rest.

Chapter 19

"I am so glad we could meet for lunch today," Faith chimed. She stared into Chrishawn's eyes like she had never seen them before. There was something magical about them that she had not seen until she let go of Gavin.

"Me too. It's rare that I can come from Oakland to San Fran for lunch. But when you made the suggestion last night, I couldn't resist spending time with you. It won't be long before we are heading back to Jacktown for the wedding and homecoming."

"Yeah, I know. I talked to Aunt Jackie again last night and everything seems to be on the up and up with her and Darnell."

"So he got all that previous marriage stuff handled?"

"Yeah, I believe so. That was straight crazy, huh? I mean his heart was in the right place, but man, he was risking a lot by doing that for that lady."

Chrishawn noticed the twinkle Faith had in her eyes. God began to show him her in a different light. He imagined walking her down the aisle. He imagined her sitting on the front pew of his church as the first lady. He saw them chasing after their kids in a big backyard. He saw their future.

"Hey, earth to Chrishawn. What are you in deep thought about over there? I am just running my mouth about Darnell and you seem to be off in la-la land," Faith said.

"Oh, God was just giving me a glimpse of our future." He smiled.

"Umm hmm, and what did you see?"

"You'll see." He grinned. He leaned in and gave her a kiss. She felt a new sense of peace. Old things were truly passed away and all things were becoming new.

"Well I am looking forward to our future, Chrishawn. I know it took me a minute to meet you at this place, but I am here now and I am happy and I am peaceful with you."

"I'm glad, Faith. We've both been through some stuff, but God," he said and laughed.

"What's so funny?" she asked.

"I talked to Chrissy this morning and I said the same thing, BUT GOD," he replied. "Those two words have a lot of weight, you know. It's like, whatever problem you have or whatever situation you are in, BUT GOD."

"Yeah, I feel you on that. How's Chrissy doing in New York anyway?"

"Oh she's doing very well. She's got a new *friend* and everything." He beamed.

"Wait, what kind of *friend*? Boy or girl?"

"Well he's not her boyfriend, but I think it's moving quickly in that direction," he announced.

"Wow, really. Who is this guy?" Faith asked excitedly.

"He's from New York...a Puerto Rican guy who has his own car service business. He was the one who picked her up from the airport when she first arrived. And those two have not parted ways since."

"What? For real? Tell me more." Faith felt herself getting caught up in Chrissy's life like she used to when they were best friends.

"Wait a minute, I forgot my rule of not talking about my sister with us."

"Oh come on, Chrishawn, your sister has been my best friend since high school."

"She *used* to be your best friend," he corrected her.

"I know. I know. But I still want to know more about this new guy in her life. This is the type of stuff we used to talk about all the time."

"Yeah, I know," he said sarcastically.

"So spill it," she begged.

"Nope, you're just going to have to rekindle your friendship and find out more yourself. She's bringing him home so maybe you can pry it out of her then."

"What!" Faith exclaimed. "She's actually bringing him home with her? Oh yeah, this dude has got to be serious."

"Yeah, I think it's pretty serious. I can't wait to meet him. Better yet, I can't wait for Mom to meet him. She's going to flip because Chrissy hasn't told her anything about this new guy." He laughed.

"Oooh, you know your mom is definitely going to trip out. She likes to be in the know, you know." Faith smiled.

The two continued to have lunch and discuss their upcoming trip home. As Chrishawn talked on and on, Faith zoned out and God revealed the exact vision he had just given Chrishawn. She smiled and without moving her mouth thanked God for helping her to move forward into the life he had planned for her.

Chapter 20

Reyna looked around the house. Everything looked perfect, again. She had taken her meds and had managed to calm down. Ever since she had stopped going to psychotherapy treatments, there were certain times she couldn't control her bipolar disorder. She felt better and couldn't wait to keep her plan in motion with Rohan's visit.

The doorbell rang and Reyna took a deep breath and smiled. She calmly walked to the door. She was totally shocked when she saw Charlotta standing there with Rohan.

"Oh, uh, hello Mr. Aguilar…Mrs. Aguilar." She paused. "I wasn't expecting you, Mrs. Aguilar."

"Surprise, Surprise," she replied in a smart-alecky tone. Rohan gave a slight nudge as if to say, don't start yet honey.

"Come on in, you guys. Make yourself at home."

"It is our home, little girl," Charlotta said, not being able to withstand the gall of Reyna Reynolds.

"Yes, that's correct. You are very much correct," Reyna stated with a plastered smile.

"So, Mr. Aguilar, you wanted to talk to me about Recio's school and this house, right?"

Rohan nervously fidgeted with his sterling silver bracelet. "Um, yeah Reyna, we need to talk to you about some things."

Charlotta cut her husband off. "Reyna where is Recio anyway?" she said while looking around.

"Oh, my sister ReRe picked him up from school today. Why?"

"Because I want to see my grandson, that's why," she replied. "How dare you even ask me why."

Rohan was about to cut his wife off, but when he looked into her raging eyes, he knew it was a lost cause. Charlotta was about to handle this deal and there was nothing he could do about it.

"Reyna, look, now that I know what's going on," she stated while giving her husband the eye, "it's time to get some things straight. First of all, Remi told us about the restaurant situation. You had no business saying those things about his wife. That's why my son lost his mind with your crazy behind."

Charlotta continued to inch up on Reyna until she had her up against a wall in the living room.

"Second of all, you had no business trying to blackmail my husband with my son's child. You living rent free in this fine house in River Oaks and we're paying for Recio's schooling and not spending a minute of our time with him. That's uncalled for.

"And third, you have absolutely lost your cotton-picking mind if you think this little game you are playing is going to continue. The buck stops here, little girl. You may have run over my poor husband because all he was concerned about was protecting Remi, but there is a new sheriff in town, my dear. And nobody, I mean nobody messes with my family, you hear me little girl? Nobody!"

By this time, Reyna was trembling. Charlotta's tall frame towered over her and she could see not escape. She darted her eyes nervously to the right and left. She noticed the knives on the island in the kitchen. She quickly ducked under Charlotta's arm and dashed into the kitchen and grabbed a knife.

"Get away from me you crazy people. All of you, just get away from me and leave me the hell alone. All I wanted was a father for my child and a lover for my soul. But nooo, you had to go and ruin my plans. First Remi is mad at me, now you two are mad at me. I can't take this anymore. I just wanted to be loved by somebody."

Reyna began to cry uncontrollably and Charlotta had given her husband the go ahead with her eyes for him to try to grab the knife from Reyna during her weak moment. But just as he reached her, she regained her psychotic state. "Get away from me or I will do it. I will cut myself!"

Charlotta saw the desperation in her eyes. This girl needed some serious help. "Reyna, please, don't harm yourself. It's going to be okay, sweetheart. We didn't mean to disturb your plans. How can we help you get what you want," she calmly stated.

You would have thought Charlotta was a trained hostage negotiator the way she calmly talked to Reyna. Those 21 hours of psychology classes back in college was starting to pay off.

"I just want somebody to love me." Reyna cried. Her tight grip on the knife was starting to ease and Charlotta once again darted her eyes from her husband to Reyna's hand.

"We love you, Reyna and we love Recio. You are our family now, honey. We're sorry that it took so long for us to come around. But things are going to be better from hence forth, okay sweetie."

"Okay, Mom. Okay, Mom." She cried.

Rohan jumped in and wrestled her to the ground and took the knife from her hands. She didn't give up much fight as she lay there on the gray tile floor crying and sobbing.

"Jesus, Rohan, you didn't have to tackle the poor girl," Charlotta scolded. "Let's call the Reynolds."

Rohan called information and got the number to Reyna's parents' home. After giving them the quick version of the story, they told him they would be right over.

"You love me, don't you Mom and Dad?" Reyna asked in between the sniffles. "You do love me, right?"

"Yes," they both exclaimed. "It's going to be all right. We are going to get you some help, okay honey. Just relax."

Rohan opened the fridge to get Reyna some water. She was sweating buckets and Charlotta suggested they go back to her room and put on something drier.

Charlotta laid Reyna down on the chaise lounge in her room and went into her closet. She started moving clothes around on the hanger and saw a glimpse of a picture. She moved the clothes back further and revealed the shrine to Remi.

She gasped and grabbed her mouth before the scream could escape. *Jesus, Jesus, Jesus. This girl does need some serious help. Help us to help her, Lord.*

෯ ෯ ෯

After having time to calm down and collect her thoughts, Giselle called Remi's cell phone. She had made her way home and noticed his truck sitting in the driveway. *What is he doing home this time of the day?* she wondered.

Remi answered the phone as she drove into the driveway.

"Baby, what are you doing home?"

"How do you know I am at home?" Remi asked, nervously peeking out the back kitchen window. He noticed Giselle's car pulling up.

"Because I am at home... I have had the worst day. You won't believe what happened. You know your friend's sister Reyna?"

Just the name made Remi cringe. "Baby, just come on in the house. This is crazy that we are talking on the cell phone and you are right outside the house."

Remi hung up the phone and took several deep breaths before Giselle walked through the back kitchen door. He nervously fidgeted with his cell phone and Giselle knew something wasn't right as soon as she walked in the door.

"Remi, what's wrong? Why are you looking like that? Do you already know what I am about to tell you?"

Remi shuffled his feet. He couldn't hide anything from Giselle. She knew him, at least she thought she knew him.

"Sweetie, I need to talk to you about something," he said and motioned for her to follow him in the bedroom. He felt it would be more comfortable there. Giselle had made it her business to make their bedroom very peaceful. She called it their sanctuary and Remi loved the fresh vanilla bean smell and the fung shui of the room.

"Baby," Remi said, "what I have to tell you is hard. I mean, I am still trying to come to terms with it myself. I will preface what I am about to say with this: It happened before I met you."

Giselle let her shoulders down in defeat. He was about to tell her what she didn't want to hear. He was about to confirm just what Reyna had told her. He was about to tell her about their child. She braced herself for the blow that was about to take their marriage to new heights. Even though she had originally told Remi whatever happened to him before they got married was his business, this old business was about to affect their lives in a major way.

In a calm manner, she spoke with the strength God gave her. "Baby, you know I am not going to trip about something that happened to you before me. How can I? That's not fair to you."

"I know, sweetheart, but I feel like I betrayed you anyway."

Here it comes, she thought. *Lord, help me.*

"Talk to me, Remi. What is it?" She pulled herself back on the bed to rest her head on the headboard. Remi followed suit. This was their normal position for conversation. They loved their bedroom chats. But this revelation was about to change everything.

"Wait a minute. You were in the middle of telling me about Reyna. I don't want to cut you off. You go first," Remi said, surprising Giselle.

Giselle replayed the nasty and insane conversation in her mind that she had had with Reyna. She wanted to hear it from her husband though.

"No, please honey. You tell me."

Remi noticed exactly what Giselle had just requested of him. Did she know, he wondered. *Oh well, everything is about to be out in the open now.*

Remi went into details and told Giselle the entire story about the restaurant episode and why he went to meet with Reyna in the first place. By the time he finished telling Giselle everything, the tears from her face were streaming non-stop. *Reyna was right. They do have a son together and I can't get pregnant.*

Remi held his wife. He felt so bad that he hurt her. He wished he had never slept with Reyna.

Through her tears, Giselle realized that Remi hadn't finished the story. He hadn't mentioned their son. He had only told her about them sleeping together.

She removed herself from his embrace. "Remi, don't you have something else to tell me? Don't you want to finish the story?"

With a look of utter confusion on his face, Remi started shaking his head slowly, yet unsurely answering no. "What do you mean, Giselle? I told you everything, honey. Is there something that *you* know?"

For as long as she had known Remi, Giselle never knew her husband to be a liar. She studied his eyes. He had no idea and she didn't want to be the one to break this big news to him. But she realized that she had no choice. This was her husband and all of this with Reyna needed to be dealt with.

"What about the baby, Remi?"

Chapter 21

Everybody was to meet up at Remi's parents' house. It had been a few days and Reyna had been released from the hospital with a new prescription from her doctor. ReRe had agreed to pick her up and drive her and Recio over to the Aguilar's house. Their parents would be there, too.

Remi and Giselle stood in their walk-in closet.

"Are you ready for this baby?" Giselle asked Remi as she noticed him readjusting his tie for the tenth time. He wanted to look his best when he met his son for the first time.

"As ready as I will ever be, G," he said with fake confidence that quickly revealed the truth. "I'm nervous, but I know that with you by my side, and my mom and dad there, I will be okay. Plus after that prayer you prayed last night, I know God is with us."

Giselle nervously smiled at Remi. Ever since he found out that he had a son, he had been restless and anxious. Giselle and Charlotta thought it would be good for the family to all meet for dinner after church on Sunday at their home. Charlotta had never met Recio either and even though she was just as excited to meet her first and only grandchild, she knew being a supportive mother to Remi was more important than anything else.

The Reynolds had been very supportive after the fiasco with Reyna. They had made plans to move Reyna in with them. They agreed it was finally time to deal with their wayward daughter and stop running from her and pushing her away.

"Well this is it, G. I always envisioned meeting my first child at a hospital surrounded by doctors and nurses and me holding your hand telling you to push, but this is just something totally different and unexpected."

"That will happen for us, Remi. One day it will. I truly believe it will. For a moment my faith wavered, but after all this, I know that God yet still has his hands on us and we will get through all of this together. I married you and this child is part of you."

"I love you, you know that, right?" Remi asked the question, but already knew his wife's answer.

"Of course I do," she replied and gave him a tight squeeze.

Remi paced the hardwood floor while waiting on Reyna, ReRe and Recio to arrive. The Reynolds had already arrived. They were talking to his parents like it was old times on the old neighborhood street, and everybody was playing it cool. That is, everybody except Remi. Giselle was helping out in the kitchen and Remi was all alone in the front room. He kept rehearsing what he would say: *Hey son, I'm your father. How's it going, son? My name is Remi and I am your father. It's me, your daddy. Son, it's your dad.*

He felt himself getting frustrated and just as he was about to pound his fist into the wall, he saw a car coming down the street. It was them. *Oh God, they are here. Lord, help me to say the right thing.*

"Giselle, Mom, Dad, I see them. They're coming," he screamed to the rest of the house.

Everybody stopped what they were doing and ran to the front room where Remi had nearly worn out his mother's Persian rug with his pacing back and forth.

They watched as ReRe helped Recio get out of the back seat. Reyna looked sick. Her meds had her looking drowsy and out of it. She slowly climbed out of the passenger side and shuffled her way to the door without even waiting for ReRe and Recio. Remi noticed how her walk had totally changed from that day at the restaurant.

The doorbell rang and Remi's heart began to race a mile a minute. "Breathe, Remi. Just breathe," he told himself.

Remi's father put his arm around his son to offer his support. Remi still didn't know that his dad had kept this secret from him. Remi had told his parents before they could tell him. Charlotta and Rohan just left well enough alone. Finding out he had a son was enough to deal with. He didn't need to know that they already knew.

As soon as the three walked in, Recio came running toward Remi. "Daddy, Daddy!" he exclaimed and jumped into Remi's arms. Remi picked him up and swung him around. "Hey there, little man."

Remi didn't have a clue as to how he knew who he was, he was just glad that Recio had prevented him from making a fool out of himself with all the ways he had rehearsed their first introduction.

As both families made their way into the formal dining room, Reyna nervously made eye contact with Giselle. She darted her eyes to Giselle and back to the floor. Giselle felt sorry for her and went over to her.

"Reyna, it's okay. I don't blame you. I know that you are not well and everything is going to be fine. We are going to be here for Recio and we are going to be here for you."

Reyna began to cry and fell into Giselle's arms. ReRe was about to come and see about her sister until Giselle silently mouthed to her she could handle it. She took Reyna into the living room and sat down with her on the sofa.

Reyna poured her heart out to Giselle. She said she was sorry about twenty times before Giselle finally cut her off. "There is no need to keep apologizing," she stated with sincerity.

Just as the family was about to sit down and eat, the doorbell rang again. Rohan went to the door to answer it.

"Sir, this package is from Boshier LLC, and I was told to deliver it to a Mr. Rohan Aguilar."

Rohan was shocked that they would be delivering on a Sunday afternoon. He stepped outside the door and signed for the package.

"Sir, we usually don't deliver on Sunday, but our office is going to be closed tomorrow for maintenance and I thought I would do you a courtesy and deliver it today. I hope that was okay."

"Yes, sir, that's fine. You guys are pretty quick."

"Well, it looks like you caught us out of peak season, so we were able to get to yours sooner than we thought. It normally takes five days for testing, but yours only took two."

"Thank you for bringing this over. I appreciate it. Have a great day."

"You too, sir. I hope that the information in that envelope tells you everything you need to know."

"I'm sure it will."

Rohan watched as the man walked to his car and proceeded to back out his driveway in one of those new electric cars. He looked inside and saw Remi playing with Rohan. He bit his bottom lip. How could he have kept this secret from his son all these years? He turned his attention back to the large white envelope and contemplated opening it. He had already caused enough grief. He opened the envelope. When he read the contents, he nearly collapsed.

Back in the house, Giselle watched intently as Remi played with Recio. She admired the way he interacted with the young boy and deep down wished that he was their child. She closed her eyes and whispered a prayer to God.

"Please dear God. Help us to have our own child one day. I know that you said in your word that we shouldn't get weary in well doing. Please help me not to get weary. Help me not to resent Remi, or Reyna for that matter, for the child they have together. Help me to be a good *other* mom to Remi's son. Let our family get along with the Reynolds and Father God help us to…" Giselle paused because she heard the front door slam really loudly.

"Charlotta, get in here. I need to show you something," Rohan nearly screamed. Even though he called Charlotta, the whole family, including the Reynolds came running to the door. Rohan was panting hard and his face looked like he was ready to kill somebody.

"What, what is it, Rohan? Why are you screaming and why are you…" Charlotta was cut off by Rohan.

"Come look at this baby. Look at this!" he shouted while thumping his index finger on the papers he had placed on the table.

Charlotta looked at the papers. She then lifted them from the table to get a closer view. She read the words over and over again. Her mouth fell open when she realized what she had read. She looked at Rohan who returned a menacing stare. She looked over at Recio who was happily playing with the orange and black ball Remi had purchased for him. She looked at Giselle, then at Reyna and ReRe who were standing there waiting for somebody to say something.

Charlotta finally broke her silence. "I can't believe this. I just can't believe this."

"Well believe it, baby. It's right there in black and white."

Now everybody was starting to get perturbed at them for not revealing what they had discovered.

Remi spoke up. "Mom and Dad, what is the deal? What is that y'all are looking at?"

Rohan gladly answered, "I will tell you what it is, son. It's DNA test results and you know what it says?"

"No, what Dad," Remi asked as he scooped up Recio who was now begging to be picked up.

"It says that that little boy you are holding is not your son."

Everybody in the room was stunned. No one moved other than Recio who was still being playful in Remi's arms.

Charlotta shook her head as she read the papers again and tried to pass them over to Remi for him to look. Before they reached his hands, Reyna jumped in between them and snatched the papers out of Charlotta's hands.

"Wait a minute. Let me see that. I know Recio is Remi's son and I don't care what this little paper says. Mr. Aguilar probably concocted this paper himself," she quickly accused.

Rohan nearly lost it when Reyna accused him of falsifying the document.

"Oh it's real. All these years, you have blackmailed me into thinking Recio was my son's child. You are…."

A confused look took over Remi's face.

"Dad what do you mean all these years? You mean you knew about Recio and didn't tell me?" Remi fumed. He felt a big lump in his throat.

"Son, what does it matter now? The boy ain't yours," he retorted. Rohan focused his attention back on Reyna. He had given her so much money and had taken care of her and Recio since he was a little baby.

"Reyna, how could you? All this time. All this time you knew he wasn't Remi's child," Rohan started back in on her.

Reyna couldn't believe what she was reading. If Recio wasn't Remi's child, then whose was he?"

ReRe stepped up and looked at the papers. She saw the hurt in her twin sister's eyes and felt sorry for her.

"Reyna, it's going to be okay. We will find out who Recio's father is, okay?"

Reyna snatched away from ReRe. She was filled with emotion and ran out the front door. The Reynolds grabbed their things and rushed out behind her. ReRe and Recio were left inside.

"Guys, I am really sorry about everything. I know my words probably don't mean much to you all, but we are really sorry about this. I have to go, but Remi, I hope that one day you can find it in your heart to forgive us.

"Mr. Aguilar, I will make sure you get back every penny you spent on my nephew and my sister. I know you all probably want to talk about this more, but I have to go and be with my family now. Again we are really, really sorry about everything. Please forgive us."

Before anyone could say anything, ReRe grabbed Recio and dashed out the door after her family. Remi looked at his father and left the room.

Rohan was about to go after Remi, but Giselle stopped him. "Give him some time, Dad," she requested. "Can you imagine being told you have a son, then being told you don't and then to find out your daddy knew everything all along? Give him some time, okay."

Giselle went after Remi. She found him back in his old room.

"Baby, are you okay?" she nearly whispered to Remi. He was sitting at his childhood desk twirling a pencil. She hugged him from behind and kissed the top of his head. "It's all going to be okay, Remi. Don't you see that God worked this out before you could even get attached to that little boy?"

"But I already feel like I am attached. I mean, for a few minutes, I was his father. I felt like his father, Giselle."

"Baby, I know. But just imagine if you had gone on for days thinking that he was yours. It would be even harder to overcome."

"And then my father lied and didn't tell me. That's something I will never get over."

"Don't say that, Remi. You will find it in your heart to forgive your dad. I am sure he had his reasons for keeping this from you. I am not sure if it's a good reason, but I am sure he had a reason."

"Yeah, I'm sure he did," Remi dryly responded.

There was a knock at the door. It was Remi's mom. Giselle ushered her in with her hand. "Come on in, Mom."

"Honey, are you okay?"

"Did you know, Mom?" Remi asked. He stared through the mirror on his desk at his mother who was now standing behind him.

"To be honest son, I just found out myself. Your father kept this from both of us. And believe me, I gave him an ear full for keeping it from me…and you. But sweetheart, he was trying to protect you and keep you focused on school. He didn't want you to drop out of school to come home and take care of a baby. I know that he shouldn't have made the choices that were meant for you to make, but you have to know that your father loves you so much and he didn't want anything to knock you off track."

As the three of them sat in the room, Rohan listened at the door. He felt horrible. His son was mad at him and he was mad at himself for not doing a DNA test when Reyna first came to him. All of this could have been avoided had he done a test back then. All of this could have been avoided had he not tried to handle this problem by himself.

Chapter 22

Jackie and Darnell's wedding day was only two days away, and JSU's homecoming weekend was right behind it. With the wedding being on a Friday evening, Jackie had arranged for the rehearsal and rehearsal dinner to be held on Thursday evening. She already had everything in order when Faith and Chrishawn arrived at Jackson International Airport from California on Wednesday morning.

"Thanks for picking us up, Aunt Jackie," Faith said as she jumped in the car and left Chrishawn outside to put all the bags in the trunk.

"Not a problem, my dear. I already have everything lined up, so I am just easy breezy right now, baby."

"So you're not nervous at all," Faith asked.

"Nope. Matter of fact, I am more than ready to become Mrs. Darnell B. Smith. It's been a long time coming." She laughed.

"Yeah right." Faith laughed back.

Chrishawn got in the car and gave Aunt Jackie a kiss on the cheek from the back seat. "So are you nervous?"

Faith and Jackie laughed as they drove away from the terminal. Chrishawn looked confused but decided to leave it alone. He knew from being the lone male with his mom and sister that he didn't even need to try to figure out what Faith and Jackie were laughing about.

Women, he thought, laughing to himself.

Chrissy loaded her bags into the trunk of Armando's car.

"Why are you doing that, my love?" Armando asked. "Let me get that for you." He rushed over to help Chrissy get her large red luggage into the trunk.

"Oh I got it. You don't have to load my bags like I am your passenger, Armando. I can load them myself."

"I will always treat you like you are my passenger and do whatever I can to be of great service for you." He smiled.

Chrissy smiled back and allowed Armando to finish putting her bags in the car.

"So is that everything?" she asked.

"Yep, I think we got all 100 of your bags and my one bag in here," he joked.

"Real funny. I can't help it if I like to shop."

"Chica, you have done more shopping for your mom and baby girl in the last few days than I have ever seen any woman do."

"Well when you go to Chinatown and see all the great deals, you can't help but grab stuff. I know my mom is going to love that orange purse I got her. She's kind of flashy like that."

"I can't wait to meet your mom. I bet she's as beautiful as you are and so is your baby."

Chrissy thought about her baby. She missed her so much. Even though she was finally getting used to living in New York and working the coolest job she could have ever dreamed of, she was missing her baby girl. Gavin had been keeping her a lot since he returned from California. It was going to be hard to have Gavin in Nashville at Meharry, her mom in Jackson, her brother in Cali, and she and baby Grace in New York, but they would have to make due and all visit each other a lot.

Armando shut the trunk and broke Chrissy out of her thoughts.

"Let's get going, chica. We have an 18-hour drive."

"Okay, let's say a prayer before we leave," Chrissy said.

Chrissy grabbed Armando's hands and the two prayed for safe travels to Mississippi.

෴   ෴   ෴

It was early Thursday morning and Remi and Giselle were boarding the plane headed to Jackson. Giselle's stomach was starting to feel queasy from the fast food she had quickly gobbled down. She hated eating on the run. Remi was glad to be getting out of Houston for the weekend to attend Jackie and Darnell's wedding and to reconnect with his college friends for homecoming. This would be a great break from the drama going on in his life.

"Baby, are you excited to be going back to Jackson? I hear that the Sonic Boom has a pretty big band this year," Giselle said trying to get her husband out of his funk.

Remi perked up. "Yeah, I heard they got it going on, baby. I can't wait to see them in action. I can't believe we are playing Southern University for homecoming. That never happened when I was there."

Giselle knew the band talk would get him going. She was married to a historically black college band geek.

"Did you remember the rental car info?" Giselle asked.

"Yep, got it right here," Remi said patting his pant pocket.

"Good. You know my dad was tripping because we were renting a car, but I told him we didn't want to inconvenience him and Mom by borrowing one of their cars," Giselle said.

"Yeah, plus we are going to be rolling. We got the wedding, then there's the Greek step show, then the parties, the tailgating and the homecoming game. I wouldn't want to put them out either."

"We are going to be so tired when we get back home." Giselle laughed. "But it will be a good tired."

Remi looked at his wife and smiled. As they glided across the skies, he had an a-ha moment. If he had come home to raise Recio, he would have never met Giselle. He couldn't imagine his life without his best friend. He closed his eyes. *Thank you Lord for working this out the way you did. Help me to forgive my dad and move forward.*

"Baby, are you listening to me?" Giselle asked as she broke into his silent prayer.

"Oh, I'm sorry, baby. I was just saying a quick little prayer. What did you say?"

"I'm sorry, I was just telling you that I can't wait to see the crew," she repeated.

"Oh me either. I saw on Facebook that Chrissy was doing well in New York. Her status said something about finding new love. I don't know what's up with that, but I am sure we will find out when we hit Jack town."

"Yeah, I had a quick direct message chat with Faith on Twitter and she said she and Chrishawn are doing well, too. That's something how those two hooked up."

"My boy Gavin is the only one who ain't hooked up with nobody," Remi said in a tone that sounded like he felt sorry for his former roommate and best friend in college.

"Well he won't have time anyway. He's about to be all up in those books," Giselle said. "Once he finishes school, then that special someone will come, but when medical school starts, he's barely going to have time for himself, let alone somebody else." She laughed.

"You right, baby. I am so proud of my boy though. He did his thing. And from his email he seems to have moved on from Faith."

"Well, it's no need of holding on to something that's not there. I'm glad he's moving on with his life. God will bless him with someone when the time is right," Giselle said with surety.

✎ ✎ ✎

"Momma, has Chrissy called yet? They're supposed to be getting here today, right?" Chrishawn asked his mother with a mouthful of Scurlocks donuts. He missed the confectionary treats only made in Jackson.

"Well let's see. I got several calls from her yesterday and they were supposed to be staying the night somewhere in North Carolina. I think she said Johnson City."

"Oh okay. Well I am going to try to call her again. I keep getting her voicemail."

Chrishawn dialed Chrissy's number again and this time his sister picked up.

"Hey, girl, where y'all at?"

"Hey, big brother. Um, I don't know." Chrishawn heard Chrissy ask Armando.

"He said we are on I-20. We just crossed the Mississippi – Alabama line. We are in some small rural town. The sign says Toomsuba." Chrissy laughed. Mississippi was known for having some weird town names.

"Oh y'all are in the deep country because I have never heard of Toomsuba." Chrishawn laughed with her.

"Toom what?" Charnese asked.

"Just tell Mom we are probably about an hour and a half away. I see a sign about Meridian, Mississippi and I know that's only about an hour from Jackson.

"All right sis, well y'all be careful. I'll see you soon."

"Cool. We'll see y'all in a little bit."

Chrissy hung up and looked up at the narrow two-lane road they were traveling on. Armando had swerved into the other lane. He had dozed off to sleep. Chrissy screamed at the oncoming 18 wheeler that was headed straight for them.

Armando woke up and snatched the wheel to the right to get back into their lane, but it was too late, the 18 wheeler clipped their car and sent them barreling down the road's embankment.

The car kept rolling. Chrissy and Armando were both screaming. Then Chrissy only heard herself screaming. The car was still rolling and landed into a pond. As the car began to fill up with water, Chrissy fought to get her seat belt undone. She wrestled with the seat belt and noticed Armando wasn't moving.

"Oh God, help us please," she cried as the car kept sinking.

She couldn't get the seat belt unfastened. She tried to roll down the window, but the power windows weren't working. She quickly tried to wake Armando, but he was unconscious. The car was starting to slowly sink into the pond head first. She took slow breaths and called on God again.

The car seemed to stop sinking. An episode of the Today show came to her remembrance. She had been home with the baby when they did a story about escaping from a sinking car. She grabbed her laptop that she had been working on earlier, and slammed it against the window. It broke the window and water started coming in even more. Chrissy again tried to unfasten her seat belt. This time it worked. She unhooked Armando and tried to wake him again. He still didn't wake up.

Chrissy heard voices as she tried to pull herself and Armando out of the car that was starting to sink again.

"I can see them from here. They're unhooked. Let's go get them out of there," she heard. Tired from treading water and pulling Armando's lifeless body, Chrissy lost consciousness and began to sink.

"Ma'am, can you hear me? If you can hear me, you are on your way to the hospital in Meridian," the paramedic said to Chrissy.

She was slowly regaining consciousness and gave him a thumbs-up. She drifted in and out and wondered how Armando was doing.

As the ambulance continued to speed down the interstate, Chrissy drifted in again and heard the paramedic talking to the other ambulance that was transporting Armando.

"Are you sure he's a goner?" asked the man with a rural tone that had a serious Mississippi twang.

"I'm pretty sure…unless they can help him at the hospital, we've done all we can do here."

"10-4, man. Let's hope our passenger is okay. If we can save one life, we've done a decent job today."

"Over and out, buddy," the driver said.

Chrissy drifted out again. Deep down she hoped what she heard was wrong.

◈   ◈   ◈

Three hours had passed since Chrishawn last spoke to Chrissy. He was starting to get worried. "She should have been here by now Momma," he fumed. "And why is her cell phone going straight to voicemail?"

"She probably can't get a signal, Chrishawn. It's going to be fine. Go on to the barbershop so you can get your hair cut. I know C-Wes can't wait to see you and catch up with you."

C-Wes had been Chrishawn's barber since he was a youngster. He had missed getting his tight lines from the barber on the west side of Jackson known as C-Wes, the best.

"All right, Momma, but as soon as she gets here, tell her to call me."

"Will do, baby. Now get on out of here before C-Wes make you wait in line."

Chrishawn made his way to the barbershop and called Faith to let her know that he would see her at the rehearsal dinner. Jackie had invited everyone to the dinner, including Remi, Giselle, Gavin and Chrissy. A simple, yet casual dinner where everyone could reconnect was how Jackie had planned the evening. The dinner was going to be held at the church's fellowship hall immediately after rehearsal.

Chrishawn finished up his hair cut and headed back to his mom's house to shower before the dinner. He was flipping through the radio stations and finally found the new gospel station.

"This is DJ Praise Man, what's your prayer request today?" the smooth voice crooned from his mother's Honda Accord speakers.

"Yes, I would like to pray for the people who were in an accident I saw on I-20 near Meridian. I don't know their names, but I know God knows who they are. I just want the listeners to pray for them."

"Okay sister, and what is your name?"

"My name is Angel Williams. I'm a truck driver and I saw this accident as I was driving into Jackson a few hours ago."

"We will definitely keep those people in our prayers. Thank you, Angel, for your call."

"Praise Family, let's pray for all the individuals involved in that accident and the paramedics and doctors who may be working on them right now. Father God, in the name of Jesus, touch them and heal them. Be in that hospital room with them. Be with everyone that has a hand in their life right now, Father. In the name of Jesus we pray, Amen."

Chrishawn listened on as the music started playing. He said a quick prayer for the people himself and continued on to his mom's house. He had not gotten a call from his mother, but he figured as soon as Chrissy and Armando arrived, his mother would have been too busy trying to meet and greet Armando to even remember to call him,

He pulled up to the house and his mother came running out with the cordless phone in her hand. "Chrishawn! Chrishawn! Chrissy has been in an accident. We have to go to Meridian Hospital."

Chrishawn paused. It felt like déjà vu. The last time his sister had been in the hospital was when she found out she was pregnant and foolishly thought she could abort her baby by taking some pain pills. Then it hit him. He had just prayed for his sister.

When they arrived at the hospital in record time due to Chrishawn's Nascar-like driving, Chrishawn ran up to the desk to ask the receptionist where Chrissy was located. It was a small town hospital and the information desk receptionist quickly told them they were in the ER.

Chrishawn and his mother made their way over to the ER and found Chrissy sitting up in the bed crying.

"Chrissy, baby, oh my God honey, are you okay?" Charnese asked.

Chrishawn went to the other side of the bed and tried to hug Chrissy, but she yelped from the pain. She was severely bruised from the accident.

"I'm fine, you guys," she said between huffs and puffs. "But I heard them say that Armando didn't make it." She let out a huge cry and put her hands to her face.

"Are you sure, Chrissy? Did they come tell you that?" Chrishawn asked.

The way Chrissy was crying for Armando, Charnese could tell he was more than a friend. She grabbed her daughter's hand and squeezed it gently. "It's going to be okay, Chrissy. Let's just make sure you are okay and then we can check on your friend."

"I'm fine, Mom. I'm bruised up, but they said I am going to be fine...nothing is broken."

"Oh thank God," Charnese replied.

"I'm going to go and see what I can find out, sis. I will be back." Chrishawn kissed Chrissy on the cheek and took off to find out what was going on with Armando. He knew how much Chrissy liked Armando, and he hoped for the best as he turned the corner heading back to the information desk.

"Excuse me again, ma'am. Can you tell me where the other person is that was brought in? He was with my sister in the car."

"You may want to talk to the doctors over in the ER. I heard somebody was DOA."

"I'm sorry, what?" Chrishawn asked the small framed woman.

"DOA means dead on arrival," she said with a solemn look and tone.

Chrishawn let out a breath. He hoped that this lady was wrong. He went back to the ER and stopped one of the doctors.

"Excuse me, sir, I am looking for my sister's friend. He was a passenger in the car with her. His name is Armando…" Chrishawn didn't have a clue what his last name was.

The doctor looked at his chart. He flipped a couple of pages and then looked up. Chrishawn could feel his heart beating through his chest. He didn't know Armando either, but he prayed that *he* wasn't the DOA the lady at the information desk was talking about.

"Armando Rivera is in room 125. He's doing pretty well, several bruises of course, but he'll be okay. I heard that your sister got him out of that sinking car. Had she not done that, I don't know if he would be alive to tell you about it." The doctor smiled.

Chrishawn breathed a sigh of relief. Then he thought about the DOA again. *Who were they talking about?*

The doctor must have been reading his thoughts. "Yeah it seems the truck driver that hit them didn't make it. According to the state troopers on the scene, your sister's car is the one that caused the accident."

"Really? I wonder what happened."

"I'm not sure, son, but your sister and that guy are pretty darn lucky to be alive with just a few scratches and bruises."

"Thanks, Doctor."

Chrishawn made his way to Armando's room. He was sitting up staring into space like someone had just told him some bad news.

"Hey, Armando, I'm Chrishawn, Chrissy's brother."

A tear fell down Armando's face.

"It's okay, man, Chrissy is all right. She's in the ER," Chrishawn said. He thought maybe Armando didn't know Chrissy's status.

"I know she is okay, but the truck driver isn't and it's my fault. I fell asleep at the wheel. I never do that. Never." He wept.

"Hey, man, I know it's hard, but you're going to be okay. God will help you move forward and deal with this in time. Do you know God?" Chrishawn asked. Chrissy had never mentioned whether Armando was saved or not.

"Well I know a little bit, but probably not enough. Tell me, can God take away this pain I am feeling deep down in my heart for the death I have caused? Can he do that?"

"Yes he can. He can do anything. He has all power in his hands. Do you believe that?" Chrishawn asked.

"I know there is a God, but I have a hard time believing sometimes. Until your sister came into my life, I really didn't think too much about God. But she always prayed before we ate and then she even prayed before we took this trip.

"There has to be a God because He kept us safe just like Chrissy prayed. But why didn't God save that truck driver?"

"I don't know why, but I do know that because of this accident your walk with God is going to be stronger. We can't always explain why things happen, but we have to look at the good that will come out of these types of situations."

"I believe. I believe God saved my life today. They told me that Chrissy pulled me out. I don't know how she had the strength to do it, but God must have given it to her. I believe. I believe. I believe," he kept saying over and over again.

Chrissy hobbled into the room as Armando kept repeating the phrase.

"You believe what?" she asked.

"I believe that God saved me today. And I want to do everything I can to repay him."

"You can repay him by serving him and worshipping him and telling others about his goodness," Chrishawn ministered.

"I know I have a lot to learn about Him, but I am willing. My life going forward will be all about getting to know the God that saved my life."

Chapter 23

"**D**early beloved, we are gathered together here today in the sign of God and in the face of this company, to join together this man and this woman."

Jackie was dressed in a simple, but elegant satin, ivory a-line dress with off the shoulder sleeves. She smiled at Darnell, who was dressed in a black tux with ivory tie, then glanced over at Faith who was dressed in a Tiffany blue halter dress that fit her just right. Faith winked back her parents and smiled. They were about to become Mr. and Mrs. Darnell B. Smith and she couldn't have been more thrilled that this day had finally come.

Faith glanced over at Chrishawn who Darnell had requested to be his lone groomsman.

He is looking so fine in that tux, she thought. She saw her other parents Tommie and Leah as they sat on the front row like proud parents.

The minister proceeded with the ceremony. Faith felt like the evening was so perfect. Jackie had outdone herself with the detailed planning for the wedding. The church was beautifully decorated with calla lilies and there were ivory lights strewn about. The church was dimly lit and the ivory lights gave you a feeling that you were outside under the stars.

All of the crew was finally there and seated together. Gavin sat on the end of one of the middle pews. He was holding baby Grace. Next to him was Chrissy. Her scarred hands were in the scarred hands of Armando. They were staring into each other's eyes as the vows were being read, hoping one day it would be them. Sitting next to them was Giselle. She beamed as she looked on at the couple. Remi, who had his arm around the back of Giselle, flanked the other end of the pew. The college friends were all back together again and it was a happy occasion.

After the wedding, everybody headed to the Jackson State University ballroom. It was in one of the new buildings on campus, and Jackie had secured the place for her reception as soon as they opened it up for alumni to use. The campus was still bustling with people who were there for the homecoming weekend. Remi and Giselle brought a change of clothes so that they could attend the step show that was starting at 10 p.m.

After the formal dance, the DJ cranked up the music and the reception was jumping. Everybody was on the floor doing the electric slide, except Armando and Chrissy. Their bodies were still too sore to try to bust a move. They sat hugged up in a corner making googley eyes at each other.

"At this time, we would like all the single ladies, all the single ladies to come to the dance floor," the DJ announced. Women from every corner of the building rushed to the dance floor. This was what the single ladies were waiting for. Faith and Chrissy joined the crowd and smiled at each other while most of the older single women jockeyed for prime positions to catch Jackie's bouquet.

"Now on the count of three, I want you to toss it, Jackie," the DJ instructed. "Be ready, ladies. You could be the next one in line for a marriage miracle like these two." He laughed.

"One, two, " he paused. "Three!"

Jackie threw the bouquet and every woman reached out for it. Chrissy jumped back because she didn't want to get mauled by the women. She was already sore enough. As the bouquet descended down from the sky, Miss Jenkins, one of the more *seasoned* women at the church pushed everybody back. But before she could grab it, her new church heels gave way to the newly waxed floor and she lost her footing. At that moment, Faith reached in and grabbed the bouquet right before it hit the floor. She held it up in victory.

"All right now, Faith," the DJ announced to the crowd with excitement. "Now let's see who you are going to marry."

"All single men, all single men please come to the dance floor. Don't be shy and don't act like you don't want a good woman in your life. Get your tired behinds out here," he playfully instructed.

The men weren't as anxious as the women. They slowly made their way to the floor and many of them were pretending to be so uninterested in the task at hand. Gavin reluctantly walked up and stood at the very back of the pack. Armando was standing on the edge of the group so that he could move out the way quickly like Chrissy had done – even though he knew it wouldn't be anything like the women. Chrishawn was in the middle around a couple of older guys.

Darnell got on one knee and slowly raised Jackie's dress to remove the Tiffany blue garter she was wearing. He pretended like he was going to take it off with his mouth before Jackie gave him a look and followed up with "Honey, please don't embarrass me."

After Darnell delicately removed the garter, the DJ began the count off. This time he didn't pause and went straight through to number three.

Chrishawn, who's only five feet, eight inches, reached for it, but it went over his head and landed in the back of the pack. Gavin had caught it. He swirled the garter around his index finger and raised his left eyebrow at Chrishawn. He smiled a competitive smile at him and looked over at Faith. She slumped her shoulders and he saw her mouth, "Oh, brother."

"All right, we have our lucky couple. Faith and…what's the brother's name?"

"Gavin," someone shouted.

Chrishawn, Chrissy, Armando, Remi and Giselle all looked on as the two met in the center of the floor to dance and take pictures. It was a wedding tradition.

"Let's give it up for the lucky couple. Who knows, we may be attending their wedding this time next year." The DJ laughed and was interrupted by a visitor to his DJ booth.

As Faith and Gavin were about to make their way off the floor, a familiar voice came on the microphone.

"We won't be attending their wedding, but you all are welcome to attend ours," Chrishawn said.

Faith's eyes were bulging wide and so were Gavin's as he was still holding her arm leading her off the dance floor.

"Faith, we've been through so much together and our hearts haven't always been with one another, but I know and I know you know, that our hearts were meant to be together forever. With all the things that transpired over these last several months, I know for sure that you are my wife and I want to declare my love for you publicly and ask you to do me the honor of marrying me."

Chrishawn removed the wireless microphone from the DJ stand and as if on cue, the DJ began to play Etta James's *At Last*. Chrishawn made his way toward Faith and retrieved the diamond ring from his jacket pocket. He had purchased the ring the same day God revealed to him Faith would be his wife. Gavin was still holding her arm. He couldn't believe what was happening. His mouth said he was over her, but his heart said something different. He wanted his Faith back and now if he didn't do something soon, she would be gone forever.

As if he had asked God what to do out loud, he heard a voice in his ear. *Let her go, my son. She's not who I have for you. I only gave her to you temporarily and now that both of you have accomplished*

all I set out for you to accomplish in your lives together, it's time to
forward march.

Gavin let Faith go and Chrishawn took her hand and got on one knee. There was not a dry eye in the room as the music continued to play and Chrishawn uttered those words again. "Faith, will you marry me?"

"Yes, Chrishawn. Yes, I will marry you."

Epilogue

"Remi, if you don't hurry up, I am going to have this baby right here in this living room," Giselle shouted. Her water had broken ten minutes ago and Remi was running around like a mad man.

"I'm coming, honey. I just wanted to call Mom and Dad so they can meet us at the hospital to pick up Gia," he replied.

Remi rushed their five-year-old daughter Gia who was dressed in her feet-in pajamas out of her room and led her and a very pregnant Giselle to the car.

"Baby, it feels just like when Gia was born, huh?"

"Remi please, I am not trying to have small talk with you. Just drive this car so that I can get to the hospital and get my epidural."

"I thought you were going to go natural this time?" he joked.

"Remi, seriously, I am about to kill you if you don't get me there soon. Your son is about to come out in this truck."

After getting his girls into the truck and buckled in safely, Remi floored it to Women's Hospital in the Houston medical center. Giselle was doing her breathing exercises just as she and Remi had practiced, but the pain was getting worse.

"Oh God, Oh God, Oh God. Remmmmiiiiii!" Giselle screamed as the pain shot through her body. Remi junior was overdue and certainly ready to make his appearance.

"We're here, sweetie. Just hold on." Remi handed the valet attendee his key and slowly lowered Giselle into the wheelchair that was waiting. He knew the routine all too well. Gia had been born here five years ago.

Gia, who was no longer sleepy after hearing her mother scream, followed closely behind her parents as they rushed to the elevator and headed to the third floor, bound for the Labor and Delivery department.

Just as the elevator doors opened, Remi's parents and Gavin was standing there to greet them.

"Hey y'all, how's my daughter hanging in there?" Charlotta asked.

"Ohhhhhhh," Giselle shouted again, signaling she was in no mood for the small talk with her mother-in-law.

"Let's get you guys on back there," Gavin said and took the reins of Giselle's wheelchair from Remi.

It had been a year since Gavin arrived in Houston after finishing up top of his class at Meharry Medical School. He was headed into his second year of residency at Women's Hospital. After he arrived at Meharry, he asked God what area of medicine he should practice. He kept having recurring dreams about the abortion he and Faith had their freshman year. Then he thought about the miracle of his daughter Grace being born after Chrissy had taken those pain pills. Those two incidences confirmed the desire he already had in his heart, to study obstetrics and gynecology.

"Man, I can't believe you are a cookie doctor," Remi joked, as he followed Gavin through the double doors.

"Come on, dude, chill out." He laughed. "And stop calling it cookie. It's a vagina and it's natural and it's miraculous how God designed women."

"Listen at you being all doctor-y," Remi said.

"I don't care what all he is being," Giselle interrupted. "I just need him to be getting that anesthesiologist up in here to give me an epidural."

Both laughed as Gavin helped Giselle get into the bed. "We got you, girl. You know I am going to make sure my best friends are taken care of," Gavin assured.

"Yeah whatever man. You better not be looking at my wife's cookie. Observe from afar, man."

Gavin shook his head and laughed as he left the room when the nurse came in. He wasn't their doctor and his shift had already ended when he saw their last name go up on the activity board after they called into the hospital. He was just staying there to take care of his friends.

Remi's parents were seated in the waiting room. Gia was curled up on Charlotta's lap and had gone back to sleep. It was three o'clock in the morning and no one knew when Remi Jr, or RJ for short, would be arriving. But according to the nurse, it would be within the hour since Giselle was almost completed dilated.

Gavin sent Chrissy a text message to let her know that Giselle was in labor. He figured she was sleep and by the time she would get the message, RJ would be born. As he clamped his cell phone back on his baby blue scrubs, he phone vibrated. It was Chrissy responding back.

WAY COOL! KEEP US POSTED. WE WILL COME UP THERE AFTER HE IS BORN.

Chrissy had been up burning the midnight oil working on details for the new location for her and Armando's car service. After reviewing the numbers, Armando had gone to bed and left Chrissy up. She was determined to get the marketing portion done, but when Gavin sent her the text message, she realized that she had fallen asleep and hadn't made any headway on the marketing.

She decided the work would have to wait and walked toward their room to call it a night. She stopped to check on Grace to make sure she wasn't sneaking to watch TV. Grace was very spoiled and going on seven-years old, you would have thought the child was seventeen the way she acted as if she was halfway grown. She couldn't help it though, being raised around Chrissy's mother who had also moved to

Houston when Armando and Chrissy decided to make Houston their home after a few years in New York.

As much as Chrissy loved New York, she really wanted Grace to grow up in the south. Plus she didn't want her to be too far from her father. So when Gavin got his residency in Houston, it was a blessing. She and Armando decided it would be a great place to open a new location for Armando's car service.

Chrissy smiled at Grace who was wildly sleeping in her pink and white polka dot decorated room. Remi had hooked them up on a great house in suburban Houston, one big enough for a whole brew of children, but she and Armando had decided to wait on having children until they got the new location set up. But soon after grand opening, Chrissy had her game plan in place. As Mrs. Rivera, she was more than ready to give her husband his first child.

She shut the door to Grace's room and headed to her favorite place—in bed next to her husband.

ക്‌ ക്‌ ക്‌

"Sweetie, wake up," Faith exclaimed as she nudged Chrishawn with force.

"What? What?" he said as he woke up in a panic and shot up in the bed.

"I just got a text from Chrissy. Giselle and Remi are at the hospital. Little Remi will be born soon."

Chrishawn relaxed his shoulders and looked at Faith. She looked so beautiful in her pure white gown. The ponytail she was sporting exposed the glow in her face. "Baby, please, it's one o'clock in the morning and unless *your* water has broken, please don't scare me like that again."

Faith laughed. "Chrishawn, you know I have two more months before it's my time to go."

"Yeah, but you never know. Babies come early and they come late. You see Giselle is late, don't you," he said with a curved mouth, which meant he was proving his point.

"Whatever." She laughed as she rubbed her belly. After four years of being Mrs. Chrishawn Jackson, Faith knew her husband all too well. "Go on back to sleep then. I will wake you up again when they text me the good news."

"If it's in the next couple of hours, baby, spare me until I wake up. I need to get all the sleep I can get now. Everybody keeps telling us to sleep now or forever hold our peace." He laughed and rolled back over on his stomach. "Plus, you know we got to get up early for the prayer breakfast. And you know the pastor and first lady can not be late," he spoke more into the pillow than to Faith.

Faith playfully rolled her eyes and continued to rub her protruding belly. Ever since she and Chrishawn founded Forward March Ministries in Oakland two years ago, their lives had changed drastically. There was always something going on at the young 500 member church. While she loved being first lady, it was a lot more work than her previous job as vice president of Elite Advertising. However, being first lady of their ministry and working in the kingdom was more rewarding than her corporate gig.

But in only a few short months, she would take on the most important position in her life, that of mommy. She leaned over, kissed Chrishawn and smiled as she looked upward. God had truly led them into a blessed place of destiny.

Readers'Group Guide

Forward March

Fon James

Discussion Questions

1. Were you shocked at the outcome of this story?
2. Did you want to see Faith get back with Gavin? Why or Why not?
3. What did you think about Reyna and her schemes?
4. Why do you think Remi's father kept the baby a secret from Remi?
5. Can a parent protect their child too much by keeping them from certain things in life like Remi's dad tried to do?
6. How did you feel when Darnell told Jackie he was already married?
7. Why was it such a struggle for Faith to let go of her past?
8. Have you ever said, "I'll forgive you, but I won't forget what you did." Is that really forgiveness if you don't let it go fully?
9. Why do you think it's hard to move forward when you've been hurt in the past?
10. Unlike the ending in *Back and Forth*, did this ending provide the closure you wanted for all the characters?

Got a question about any of the characters or want to make a comment about the novel? Email the author at fon@fonjames.com.

To purchase additional copies of this book, visit www.fonjames.com or request it wherever books are sold. Also available at all online book retailers.

Printed in the United States
221823BV00001B/1/P

9 780979 957123